D1528123

WITHDRAWN

The Tennis Player

ILLINOIS SHORT FICTION

Titles in the series:

Rolling All the Time by James Ballard

Love in the Winter by Daniel Curley

To Byzantium by Andrew Fetler

One More River by Lester Goldberg

Crossings by Stephen Minot

The Tennis Player by Kent Nelson

A Season for Unnatural Causes by Philip F. O'Connor

A Horse of Another Color by Carolyn Osborn

Small Moments by Nancy Huddleston Packer

Curving Road by John Stewart

Such Waltzing Was Not Easy by Gordon Weaver

The Pleasures of Manhood by Robley Wilson, Jr.

THE TENNIS PLAYER

and Other Stories by

KENT NELSON

UNIVERSITY OF ILLINOIS PRESS

Urbana   Chicago   London

"The Tennis Player," *Michigan Quarterly Review,* Spring, 1975.

"Looking into Nothing," *Transatlantic Review,* Spring, 1975; selected for the Martha Foley collection, *Best American Short Stories, 1976*

"Incident in the High Country," *North American Review,* Fall, 1974.

"To Go Unknowing" was first published in the *Sewanee Review* 82 (winter 1974). Copyright 1974 by the University of the South. Reprinted by permission of the editor.

"By the Way of Dispossession," *Southern Review,* Fall, 1976.

"The Clay Urn," *Michigan Quarterly Review,* Spring, 1974.

"The Humpbacked Bird," *Virginia Quarterly Review,* Summer, 1975.

PS
3564
E46
T4

Library of Congress Cataloging in Publication Data

Nelson, Kent, 1943–
  The tennis player and other stories.

  (Illinois short fiction)
  CONTENTS: The tennis player.—Looking into nothing.
—The man who paid to sleep. [etc.]
  I. Title.
PZ4.N4273T3 [PS3564.E46]   813'.5'4   77–10449
ISBN 0-252-00678-X
ISBN 0-252-00677-1 pbk.

For Nona,
who helped me

Contents

The Tennis Player   1

Looking into Nothing   14

The Man Who Paid to Sleep   25

Incident in the High Country   38

The Mad Artist's Dream of Hues   48

To Go Unknowing   58

Every Day a Promise   79

By the Way of Dispossession   89

The Clay Urn   102

The Humpbacked Bird   113

The Tennis Player

A simple motion made from the shoulder. His left hand, holding the ball, came to the left knee, and, as the weight of his body shifted forward over the baseline, Nicky's arm swung upward in an arc. Suddenly the tennis ball appeared against the blue sky, like a moon rising. Through years of practice, countless tosses, Nicky saw only the ball.

It hung there, poised, and in the precise moment before it fell again, the crack of his racquet sent it away. Nicky forced himself halfway to the net, but he lunged more than ran. Agee sliced the ball back. It came high and long, and Nicky paused a split second trying to decide whether it would go out. It had been too long since he had last played to know by instinct. His pause was his decision, and he let the ball sail. It struck the court just beyond the baseline, out.

He turned a moment in Agee's direction, smiled at luck, and then walked back to the fence where the ball had stopped rolling. His smile faded. With a familiar motion, he dribbled the ball from the court onto his racquet. He could still do it effortlessly, and no stranger could tell that he had been away. He tossed the ball lightly from the racquet face to his left hand and stepped to the baseline left of center.

When he was younger, twelve and thirteen, Nicky had had tantrums on the court when the ball would not do as he wished. He cried when somebody cheated him. He remembered that well. He always read the lines honestly himself, and he could not keep other people's falseness from bothering him. Sometimes, when he lost on cheating, he broke his racquet on the ground, but it was only out of love for the game. That's how he explained it to his father.

"You can work out a new one in the store," his father said.

"But he cheated," Nicky protested.

"Two hours every day," his father answered. "You can still play your tournaments on the weekends."

Dressed in a black robe, he moved lights into position for sittings. He knew cameras inside out, knew every trick of freezing a face into a tedious smile. He knew the smells of the chemicals as the faces emerged onto cardboard in the trays. The ultraviolet lights, enlargers, dryers. He knew the faces of women and newlyweds when at last they returned to the store to collect their own images.

The ball hung, and Nicky served the first ball into the tape. The second, topspinned, turned oval in the air, thudded on the court, and bounced high and away to Agee's backhand. The return came to his left, and Nicky reached out awkwardly, out of position for such a hard shot. The ball skipped by, and he stopped short. Without expression, he turned and walked back again to the baseline. Agee lobbed a second ball over.

Nicky thought of his father's saying that the King of Sweden played tennis until he was eighty years old. His own movements came so strangely, dreamlike, as though he were so old. He told himself that he could not expect too much. But the last was an easy ball, one he should never miss.

He remembered Agee differently. Agee had seemed slower when they had played before, and he had been more cheerful. Now his friend seemed farther away, not certain anymore.

The ball always seemed beyond reach. He started to think of the way Agee had lured him out to play. Then, he thought, perhaps it had been Caroline.

"We all imagine what you've been through," Caroline had said to him.

They had sat on the swing in the warm spring night. Before they had often sat there. The terrace overlooked a long, wide swath of lawn which extended down in the dark trees and the night.

"We try to understand as best we can. All of us. But, Nicky, you can't close us out. You have to try as well. You have to try to come back to us."

He had closed his eyes and had thought then: And how did one go about coming back to everything? Yes, he wanted to come back. There was nothing he wished more than to come back into everything just as he had left it. But, happier. He had been so tired then.

He opened his eyes again to the night. "It's just that everyone has not moved at all, and I've moved a great distance," he said.

His mind went on, and he spoke as though she would know what he talked about.

"Suppose," he had said, "that I decide to do only one thing for my whole life. What happens then?"

"Why, then you become something," she said.

He remembered that he could not quite see her eyes as she had said this.

"At least you've started something," she went on, "if you make a decision like that."

"And what if the one thing you decide upon turns out to be without value?"

Caroline had looked at him. She stopped the movement of the swing by putting her foot on the ground. For a moment he thought she might be angry at such nonsense, but as she leaned forward into the light from the windows of the house, he could see in her eyes that she did not understand. She had never thought of such things. Hers was another world—one of application, restraint, and respect for property.

She did not answer his question. Instead she leaned closer to him and put a kiss on his lips.

Then her mother came outdoors. "Nicky, it's Agee on the phone. He wants to play tennis with you."

Caroline got up. "Tell him you will, Nicky."

"I'm too tired."

"You aren't really too tired."

Not really, he thought. Who knew what "really" meant? He did. It was lying in a place which was not home and wishing you were not as you were and being so lonely with so many people around you.

"No," he said. "I don't want to."

"This is what I mean, Nicky," she pleaded. "You've got to come back to us."

In the end he had agreed to play.

The first time was over. Nicky zipped the cover over his racquet.

"You can see the shape of the old self," Agee said, coming over.

"Nearly invisible," Nicky said.

He sensed Agee's hesitance to walk with him. They headed for the clubhouse.

"Later in the summer we'll play tournaments again," Agee said.

Nicky remembered the days when they had travelled the state like circus sideshow performers, playing before the crowds. The crowds were never quiet. They cheered losing shots, and always expected the favorite to win.

"No tournaments," Nicky said. "That's over."

Nicky stopped on the lawn. Caroline came down from the clubhouse toward them. She looked bright, her blond hair against the green of the trees. She twirled a daisy nervously in her hands.

Everything at the club looked perfect—the spacious lawn, the trees, the big clubhouse—while the rest of the world had to make do.

"I watched," she said cheerfully. "You both played very well."

He had looked for her car before they had gone out on the court. She must have come later. "Hello," he said, taking her hand.

Her blond hair fell to the sides of her face. She turned to Agee. "He'll soon be playing just as well as ever, won't he?"

She said he would be, he thought, precisely because that was what she was least certain about. He felt like an invalid who had to be walked and talked.

They said to him, "Nicky, look at the light."

He looked at the light. He was sure he had looked at the light. It was a small point. The voices came from their skulls, not from their mouths, as though they were in a cavern.

"Nicky, look at the light."

He was sure he looked at the light, but they kept repeating it.

Caroline looked at home in the clubhouse. "I've ordered lunch," she said.

They went in. Nicky looked around at the glass. It was an aircon-ditioned room and it felt cold. There seemed to be glass everywhere.

On a table he saw a stack of magazines. That was what had done it before, and seeing them startled him. Before, he had stopped reading newspapers and watching television and looking at magazines.

Mr. Davidson, the club chairman, came over to shake hands.

"Good to see you back, Nicky," he said.

Nicky nodded. It was as though he were back from the war, except that if he had come back from the war, their enthusiasm would not have been guarded.

"Looked pretty good out there, I must say."

"Look at the light."

The light came from a point in the flashlight.

"That's fine, Nicky."

In the beginning he had seen the light, but then, as they said "Fine," he had not. He did not feel himself move.

"Look at the light again. Over here."

He did not move.

"That's very good, Nicky. You're getting much better."

Mr. Davidson held onto his hand like an old uncle.

"I wish it felt good out there," Nicky said.

Caroline moved off with Agee.

"Nicky," Mr. Davidson said, "I have a favor."

Caroline and Agee had gone off to leave the two of them alone.

"Maybe it will help you out, too," Mr. Davidson went on. "Damon, the club pro, can't take his lessons in July. He has that clinic in Jennings, and we need someone to take over for him for a while."

Caroline was sitting down at a table, looking at him. He could see that she knew what their conversation was about. He saw her mouth moving in pantomime, "Say yes."

"Look at the light, now, Nicky," they had said.

"Looks different now," Nicky had answered.

It was still that point of light, but now he could smile when he saw it. It looked very clear.

"You're going to be home pretty soon."

"I know."

"Have you made any plans?"

"Not really. I thought I would stay around home for a while."

"What about tennis?"

"Maybe play a little tennis again and think about what's ahead."

"It would mean ten dollars an hour plus the pro shop," Mr. Davidson said.

"I haven't played at all," Nicky said.

"You haven't forgotten," Mr. Davidson said, smiling.

"It's like riding a bicycle," Nicky said, "but it's rusty."

"Well, it's only lessons. It won't be hard for you."   He saw Caroline at the table.

Tennis used to be just young days running in the sun. Now it was not.

"I'm sort of at loose ends," Nicky said. "It would help me out." He looked at Caroline.

"Good," Mr. Davidson said. "Then we're all set."

At eight every morning in July he was on the court in sneakers, white shorts, and white shirt. The sun burned him. In slow motion he demonstrated the strokes of the game to children and ladies: forehands with the handshake grip, reaching toward the net on the follow-through; backhands with the elbow locked at the moment of impact; serves like throwing the racquet over the net without letting go. He watched the awkward movements of the women, the uncontrolled hitting of the children; he listened to them laugh.

From the moment he had agreed to teach, Nicky began something new with the people around him. He had given in to telling people what they wanted to hear. Of course in the details of the senses he was scrupulously honest. He did not charge people too much on their lessons or say that shots were in which were truly out. He just did not tell them everything. He did not tell people what would hurt them. It was easier to omit.

"I don't mind the work," he said to Caroline.

"Really, Nicky?"

He did not mind the work. It was the feeling that he got from it that he could not stand.

Sometimes Caroline came out to meet him for lunch. They sat in the snack room where instants of his former life were hung on the walls: his arm around Agee after the state finals; another of the sectionals. He looked at his own tedious smiles.

"You ought to try another tournament," she said once. "Just for your confidence."

"Maybe I will," he said. He knew he could not.

At two he met a class of young boys. Caroline loved to watch the children. She sat beyond the fence on a green bench, laughing as the boys ran wildly over the courts. Nicky knew a few would become good if they played. But he could not wait that long. Ball after ball he hit to weak backhands, making sure the ball bounced to the perfect spot. "Watch the ball," he repeated over and over. "Racquet back sooner. It's too late when the ball is already there."

Caroline was the only respite, and yet he knew it was she he could never come back to. He spent most evenings with her, sitting and talking idly. He did not tell her he loved her. She believed he loved her without words, and he let her believe. He decided that at times he did love her, but since it was only at times, he knew he did not.

Sometimes they made love. Those were the times that all else faded from his mind, even the terrible light. He knew she wanted no other than him, and he tried to make her see that he had no other than her. He held her, knowing that for him there was no other chance.

He could feel that the sheets were clean. They looked tan behind her hair. Though Caroline was there in the darkness under him, he did not think of her. He knew that what he did was the worst thing he could do. Yet it was all he had, all he could do.

He knew it was not so much her, not so much being inside her body. It was being simply inside, lost within someone else, all thought concentrated outward. It was the end of having to think. It was terrible to have it not last forever, to awake and find the world more pale and less tenable than ever.

Always the next day he was back on the court with the children. He tried to vary his method, but it was not his method which lacked. Sometimes his mind wandered to the hospital where he had been tucked away from all of them, beyond the vision of all else, the all-else unknowing that it was to blame.

His mother used to say to him, "Nicky, are you well? You don't look well."

"No, I'm not."

"You don't look at all well."

"What do looks have to do with it?"

He would go down to the photography store to freeze those smiles. He knew that his was the equal of any of those terrible expressions. He went on from day to day, as if on a tightrope, the fear of falling increasing as the tightrope became looser and looser: the cars taxes directions space flights schedules discussions airplanes motels counters colors money neon swimming pools success government medicines advertisements driving him on and on over the loose rope.

He stood in one spot on the court, leaning over his basket of tennis balls, throwing hitting talking, "Careful, watch. Now follow through."

The long summer seemed to be made of the same weather, always hot air and blue sky. The sky seemed to open outward and beyond. Nicky baked to a deep brown; his hair lightened.

Damon did not come back to take over his teaching in August, but it did not matter then. When Mr. Davidson asked Nicky whether he would stay on, Nicky accepted. "I'll be glad to," he said.

Nicky never began to believe himself what he knew everyone else inferred from what he said. He was too removed and watched himself too closely. He did not make his world over into happiness. He drifted, not bothering to explain.

Toward the end of August, he began to live through the days. It seemed to him like a great eternity, each day adding to the others to make a dark pall, like velvet.

Each day he thought he would fall. But Caroline said, "You look so much healthier being out in the sun. You're much more like your old self, Nicky."

"I am myself," he said.

"Look at the light."

He could see the point of light, but he could not move.

"Do you think you might try a tournament? Just a small one?"

"I think I might," Nicky said. "We'll wait and see when one comes up."

He often told Caroline that he would be delayed at the club and that he could not come over to her place until later. This was true, but not for the reason he knew she would believe. She would think that he had a late lesson, or that the accounting of the shop had to be checked. But it was not for those reasons, or for any other that he imagined she would see.

It was only that he wanted to be alone after the club was empty.

The club was a perfect place. In the evening the courts were no longer sprayed with tennis balls; he did not have to watch shouting children as they raced after the balls; he did not have to say anything to anyone.

The club grounds were so peaceful in dark green. The air was filled with the sounds of crickets and breezes. Dusk came slowly.

One evening in late August, he stayed after lessons. He lay stretched out on the grass beside the courts. He stared through the sky, watching the light blue shade darken toward violet. The trees above him wavered and turned slowly to darkness. Stars began.

He loved watching the sky, imagining how deep it was and how it was filled up with space. His loose rope hung over that space. It seemed to him then that it would be peaceful, that fall, going through the space of the sky.

The world moved through several hours.

In this peace a motor sounded somewhere far down the gravel drive. The headlights of the car struck the leaves over his head, breaking the trees into shadows as the car moved down toward the clubhouse. He sat up. As the car turned into the parking lot, the beams moved across his white tennis clothes. He recognized the car as Caroline's.

The door slammed, and he lay back. Her footsteps across the grass drowned all the other sounds.

"What are you still doing here?" she asked. "I thought you had to go home tonight."

"I told you my mother asked me to come."

"But you didn't go?"

"No."

"I just called there and your mother said they hadn't seen you. We thought something might have happened."

She sat down on the grass beside him, folding her dress under her.

"You didn't come to me either."

"I've been here lying on the grass," Nicky said.

He nearly started to tell her how the sky seemed to go on forever, not in imaginable time, but in a way he could not even imagine, just deep and deeper.

Instead he said, "I would have come by to see you later."

"When you weren't home I was worried," Caroline said. "I had to see you."

He could not see her eyes. He thought that whenever it was important to see her eyes, they were sitting in the dark.

Something new was in her voice. Nicky turned on his side toward her. The sun from the day still swarmed in his skin. His legs felt numb and heavy. He didn't want to think about what it might be that she had to tell him. He started to reach out and touch her.

"Agee called and said I should talk to you about the tournament coming up," she said. "He thinks it might bring you back."

He knew it was not what she had come to say.

"What about my lessons?"

"It's just a tournament in the city. A small one."

"I mean, my lessons were supposed to bring me back, too," Nicky said.

"You are back, Nicky. But you don't want to go on giving lessons forever. You're a top player. Lessons aren't in you, but this is. Nicky, please."

All he could think of was falling through that endless dark space.

"Okay," he said.

That space. He reached for her and began stroking her bare arm. He heard her breath start, and he moved over closer to her. He did not want to hear what she had to tell him.

Nicky began hitting with Agee for an hour and a half every day. Caroline had signed up for an hour lesson right before lunch and gave up her time for their practice. Nicky took a half hour of his own.

Agee was good to him. Nicky started off riveted to the same spot on the court, as though it were a lesson. He could not adjust to Agee's hard shots.

"I can't," Nicky whispered over and over.

He made countless mistakes. He no longer watched the ball, but instead hit out of forgotten skill. He did just what he belabored in lessons to his students. Agee encouraged him and took it all.

After two weeks of practice, Nicky began to see the signs. His legs felt more elastic. His instincts improved; he knew where the ball would come. He started following his serve to the net with a series of quick little steps. The serve itself he whittled deeper into the service court, a little closer to the corners.

Caroline also came to watch.

"You must see the improvement from day to day," she said, when they had come from the court.

"*I* see the improvement," Agee joined in, wiping the sweat from his face. "I don't think the lessons have hurt you. You were only lazy."

Nicky smiled. He knew it was coming back. He felt the solid stroke of the racquet when he hit. He was trying shots that had been dormant for a year and a half: short topspin crosscourts, drop-shots, backhand volleys to the deep corners. They had begun to fall.

Even his mood during lessons picked up. He was less bored, and more enthusiastic about the game. "Weight always forward," he urged. "Step into the ball. Never backward."

Only one thing held him back: Caroline.

Every day she was there, not pressing him in any way, but there. She seemed to hang close to him, always at his side, and yet she did not have the same cheer in her. She seemed wary of everything he said.

"Tell me the truth, now, Nicky," she said. "What are you doing to-night?"

"I *am* telling the truth," he said.

"You're not planning anything?"

"No. Why are you like that? Because of the other night?"

He had thought about his omissions.

"No," she said.

"Look, I only wanted to isolate myself to think," he said. "I had to be alone because then I'm not lying to anybody."

"You don't have to explain anything," she said. "I understand."

"You don't understand. It wasn't only you."

"Now look here at the light, Nicky. Over here."

The point of light seemed very far away. The voices came from space. He tried to move.

"So you're back, Nicky. What happened out there? Look at the light."

"And now you think your life has purpose again?" Caroline looked at him closely.

He could see that her eyes were ready to cry.

"You said yourself that I had to start somewhere with one thing."

He knew tennis was not it.

Then the tears came. Nicky could see no reason, but he knew that reasons were not often seen. She rushed up to him and put her arms around him and held. It was the way he often held her, except that he could never cry.

Before every tournament match in the old days Nicky had had a ritual. He would sit by himself for half an hour in some quiet place and concentrate. He would hold his fists tightly closed for a minute at a time, pounding them slowly and soundlessly against his knees. He would tell himself to watch the ball and to hit hard without being nervous. He tried to relax. And he told himself that, if he got behind, he should change his strategy. Before each serve he had to bounce the ball three times for luck. And if he were winning, he should never think he had won until the last point was played.

The hour before this tournament, Nicky knew that he was not in the old days. As before he went off by himself, but he did not think about relaxing or about any of the other things.

He had been with Caroline the night before. She had been quiet, sitting there on the swing. From the step where he sat, he could look down the pathway. He listened to the crickets.

"Come sit with me," she had said.

He had not moved. He could sense in her voice that it was finally coming. "What do you have to tell me?" he asked.

In a suddenness he had not expected, the words broke from her— a child, Nicky, a child—and for a long time he sat listening to the darkness. He saw himself growing dimmer and dimmer like the fireflies far away on the lawn, and he had gotten up and started walking out toward the dark trees.

Later, sometime during their lovemaking, he had told her that he loved her. It was not any kind of omission. He knew he had had to say it. He could not stand the dishonesty, but there was no chance anymore to come back.

"Look at the light now, Nicky."

He did not see a light.

"What was it, Nicky?"

He could not feel himself move.
"The light is over here. What was it?"
He could not speak. The space seemed to close around him.
"Was it the lies, Nicky?"
He did not see anything.

He took his racquets out to the court. In the warmup he hit the ball as if he were concentrating. He knew his opponent from years before and Nicky was certain to win easily. He moved mechanically around the court, reacting without thinking.

Nicky took eight practice serves. Then he stepped up to the line and bounced the ball three times. It was his old lucky way. Then he leaned back and pointed his racquet toward the net.

A simple motion from the shoulder. The left hand, holding the ball, came to the left knee and, as the weight of his body shifted forward over the baseline, Nicky's arm swung upward in an arc. Suddenly the tennis ball appeared against the sky, like a moon rising. Years of practice and countless tosses had taught him, but now the ball seemed to disappear before his eyes, and all he saw was the wide, deep expanse of space.

Looking into Nothing

The truck brought up dust as it bounced over the roadless flat land. It pulled up near where two men were already standing by the edge of a deep canyon. Barry watched the west-falling sun turn the dust red in the air. The motor died and Turner got out.

"Where's he at?" Turner asked, coming up to the two men.

Barry turned away.

The other man, John, the oldest of the three, answered. "Down there," he said, pointing toward the draw.

Turner walked to the edge. He was a graying man, short and deeply tanned. He had the air of an investigator. "What's he doing?"

"Barry said he heard him crying. I didn't hear anything."

"You hear him?" Turner asked the younger man.

Barry took off his cowboy hat, smoothed out his long brown hair, and snugged the hat back on his head. It was a nervous gesture he made sometimes around people. "Yes, I heard him." He said the words as though his honesty were doubted.

"Where is he exactly?" Turner was used to the tone of his men.

Barry faced around. He directed Turner's gaze to the stand of aspens in the bottom of the draw. "About in the trees there," he said.

Turner shielded his eyes from the low sun. John, too, heavy and slow, stepped to the edge and raised his hand against the sun. The draw was steep-sloped, hollowed out of the flat-topped mesquite land by centuries of storm water rushing through. Below them the aspens and the grassy bottom were already in heavy shadow.

"He go down at the end?" Turner asked.

"Not really any other way. I wouldn't have known he was down there except that I heard him."

"Maybe you heard something else," John said.

Barry shook his head. "Sounded like crying."

Turner stepped away from the edge. "How long has he been gone?"

John looked at his watch. "Hour, two hours since I told him."

"That why he's down there?"

"'Course that's why," Barry said roughly. "John shouldn't have said anything."

"I just told him what everybody says. Even Turner." John looked at Turner.

"You shouldn't have told him the way you did," Barry said.

Turner tried to break in. "Well, he never knew the boy was going to do this."

"It's his own fault," John added, turning away from the edge, too.

Barry stayed out near the edge of the cliff overlooking the draw.

"What are you going to do?" he asked, looking back toward Turner and John.

"I'm not going to do anything," Turner said.

"You just can't talk to him like that," Barry said more quietly.

John eased his stance, but it made him look more defensive. "I tell you I didn't know the boy was going to run off." John spoke more to Turner. "It was just plain language, same as any other."

"Not to a man like Rail."

Turner looked from one to the other. "It's done," he said. "It wasn't anybody's fault."

The men stood waiting. The sun slipped beyond the horizon and the flat land was suddenly all gray light, the same as the light in the bottom of the draw. Without the sun the air started to cool.

"What do you suggest?" Turner asked, coming over once again to the edge.

"I think we ought to get him out."

They all knew it would not be easy to get down into the draw. The upper end was the only way, and it was a steep pitch of rocks and loose dirt. The sides were impossible without a rope.

"Maybe he's already gone down," John said. "We couldn't have seen him if he had."

"If he's gone down, we'd never find him," Turner said.

They meant that it was possible for Rail to have gone down the length of the draw four or five miles to where the draw opened out onto the river.

"Anyway, the boy knows the way home," John said.

John's words hung in the air. There was no need for anyone to say that Rail wouldn't come back home alone.

"Call down to him," Turner said to Barry. "See if he's down there."

Turner backed off. Barry stood out on the very edge and cupped his hands around his mouth.

"Rail! Hey, Rail! It's Barry. You down there?"

The voice echoed from the other side of the draw. Barry waited for the voice to dissipate.

"Rail, listen, we want you to come out. We'll help you."

The echo died.

"You down there? Come on, answer up!"

"He's not down there," John said.

Barry looked down. The sound of his voice had stopped. He could see the leaves of the aspens shaking white and then dark in the last light, like the changing sparkles of sun upon moving water. The aspens made a slight sound.

"Rail, we want to do something. John's sorry. We want to help you get out." There was a half-hearted quality in Barry's voice which belied his feeling. He turned around.

"He's down there," Barry said.

"Listen, I'm not sorry. I didn't do anything." John's voice was loud and angry and brought an echo.

"Shut up," Barry said.

The two men looked at one another. John's heavy frame seemed to make his gray eyes small and pouched. Barry felt the heat rise into his face. He took off his hat and smoothed his hair again. He saw himself, for a moment, as though outside himself, looking at his own gaunt features and dark eyes.

They had worked too long together to feel hatred, but neither of them was above fighting when angered.

Turner stepped in. "If he's down there," Turner said, "he's not going to answer."

For a moment they all stood there, not knowing what to do. The sky was an even, darkening blue-gray, without a cloud. From the top of the rim it stretched across the mesquite land for miles around.

"We might as well go on," Turner said at last.

"And leave him?" Barry asked.

"There's nothing wrong with spending a chilly night once in a while," Turner said evenly. "Won't hurt him."

"I'm not worried about the night," Barry said. "I'm worried about Rail."

"What's there to worry about? He can come home," Turner said.

"I'm worried about what he's thinking."

"What can he be thinking?" John asked. It was the first thing he'd said since Barry had told him to shut up.

For a long moment Barry didn't answer. He just stood and looked at them. His anger had gone. He couldn't help it. "You two go on back," he said at last. "I'll stay out here for a while and talk to him."

Turner sighed. "Okay," he said.

The two of them turned to go back to the truck. Barry watched them go. Then he called out, "John?"

"Yeah?" John stopped.

"Maybe you'd better wonder what he's thinking down there. If you don't know, it might help you."

John stood for a moment. Barry could see his graying form against the sky. Finally, without saying anything, John turned and walked to the truck. Turner had already started the motor and turned on the lights.

Somewhere below, in the dark stand of trees, Rail was sitting. Barry imagined the young man sitting and not walking. He imagined the difference between the broad sky which he could see from the rim of the draw and the black-bordered sky which Rail could see from the bottom.

Barry tried to listen for Rail's crying. He had heard it so clearly before, when he and John had first come to look for Rail. John had gone up the mountain, while he had come down to the edge of the draw. There had been no breeze. The aspens had been limp. It was a low moaning sound he had heard, brought up short with breaths. Barry had called out once, softly, "Rail?" and the low moaning had stopped.

The night seemed to hang over the draw. The shapes of the trees below merged with the ground, and Barry could distinguish only a vague outline of the rocks bordering. The draw seemed to flow downward, as though filled with a dark water.

He sat down on the edge of the rock and took out a cigarette. The air had cooled, but it was not yet cold. Barry knew the early morning would be the coldest time, around four or so when the dew would fall. He lit the cigarette, wondering whether Rail could see the light from the match where he sat.

He did not know why he was so certain that Rail had not gone down the draw toward the river. Rail knew the draw and knew where it went, even if he'd never walked the whole length of it. It was true that Rail was slight, and not as strong as most men. A hundred and thirty pounds. Barry smiled, thinking of Rail's thinness. Skinny as a rail. But Rail was more than that. Barry had seen him determined, and if Rail wanted to make it down, he would have done it.

Barry stared down into the blackness. "Rail?" The voice, disembodied, came back.

"It's all right, Rail, you don't have to answer. Just listen to me. I'll talk slowly or play a little, and you can listen."

Barry took a harmonica from his shirt pocket, dusted it, and then played for a minute. He carried the harp with him everywhere and often, when he had a moment alone, he would take it out for his own pleasure. He stopped the fast tune he had been playing, and then started in on "Shenandoah." When he finished, he spoke out into the darkness.

"Now you listen," he said in a steady voice. "I'm going to sit out here with you for a while. Maybe I'll play a little and maybe I'll talk, but I'll be here."

He played "Oh, Susannah." The notes slid into the stillness and kept coming back. As he played, he looked down into the draw and then at the sky. The stars were out by the thousands. He played another refrain and then stopped. The silence seemed welcome.

"You know, when I was a kid," he said in the same steady voice, "I did some pretty funny things. Not things to laugh at, but strange things. I never knew where I was going the way you do. You do know, Rail. Sure, you run into people like John. Even Turner to some extent. But they aren't holding you back. You won't be here forever. You know what you want."

From across the draw and far beyond, the howl of a coyote went up. It yapped as if wounded.

"Sounds almost better than me on my harp," Barry said. He paused to listen again to the hollow whine. "You know, that's what I was like when I was younger. I was like one of those damn coyotes. Couldn't do anything by myself. I was always too scared. I'd howl when I was alone, though. It isn't necessary to sing to the stars. I wasn't practicing for anything."

Barry paused another moment. The coyote had stopped. Looking at the stars, he absently picked out the Dipper and traced a line with the cup stars to the north. "Stars are something, huh? Never see them often enough."

He didn't know whether Rail was listening, but he did not stop. He had a certain faith that he was, and that was all he needed.

"I had a boy once." The voice was strong. "No one else at the ranch knows that I had a boy. It's one of those things that you keep hidden from the people you're around every day. Sort of like a secret only much more severe. Like a dream, too, only more real. The boy's mother doesn't even know that I know about my own son. I read it in the newspaper when he was born." Barry laughed and then was silent for a moment, thinking. "Maybe you'd think she was an ugly bitch to go with someone like me. But she wasn't ugly. I met her when I was still living in the city. She was a beautiful woman. I know you'll ask why she went with me."

He waited, as though expecting the question to come of itself from the draw.

"I can't answer why. I met her in a bar where she didn't belong. I was sitting at a table and she came up to me. She could have had anybody else, I tell you. She just came up to me. At first she didn't say anything. She just came up pretty close and stared at me. I've never seen a look like that anywhere else."

Barry caught himself. He sensed that his voice was getting too loud, and he calmed himself down. "You know me, Rail. Nothing too pretty to look at. My mouth's too big and thick, and my face is too long. I could use some weight just like you, and my hair's never combed down. But she picked me. If I'd have been in my right mind, I might have wondered why at the time."

For a long time Barry was silent. He looked at the pelting of the sky. He could remember having often seen the stars as thick as they were that night. But never before had he understood the great depth of the blackness behind the stars. It was like looking into nothing. Neither air nor color, but nothing. It hurt him to look at the sky like that.

He started out again in an uneven voice. "Sometimes you go, too. I mean, you, Rail. Sometimes your feeling is all gone. I've seen that in you before. Like that evening when Lavern came down." Barry laughed strangely in the night. "Remember? Lavern said she was going to see to you. You believed her. And then she didn't so much as look at you. Well, that's just what happened to me here as I was looking at the sky. It's as though you understand once and for all what you're all about." He laughed again. " 'Course the next morning you've forgotten it again. And that's lucky."

He stopped looking at the night sky and took out his harmonica again. He played a fast tune, sliding up and down the scale, letting the sound out with his hand. He stopped suddenly in the middle.

"I know you didn't forget Lavern. I know it got to you, and I know you did something about it. That's the way you are."

He played a train on the harp, starting slowly in the distance, speeding up and getting louder, and ending with a whistle.

"Hey, how was that?"

He expected an answer. The draw remained as dark and as silent as the blackness behind the stars.

"Rail?"

" 'Rail?' "

"You down there, Rail?"

" 'You down there, Rail?' "

"All right."

" 'All right.' "

Barry took out another cigarette. A breeze blew out the first match, but the second stuck.

"I'll stay out here with you all night, Rail," he said, back again in his even voice. "Wish I knew that you were all right, though. Wish I knew that you wanted me to. Night isn't so long that I can't stay out here."

A breeze came up again. Barry looked around him to see whether anything was with it. Nothing. Neither a cloud nor a moon. He stood up and buttoned his jacket. Then he sat down again with his back toward the breeze.

"She took me," he said, a little louder against the sound of the wind. He could hear the rustle of aspen leaves down in the draw. "She took me right out of my seat with my beer not even half drunk. That's the way my boy was begun. A night like that. I found out later what she was. Do you know?" He laughed again, nervously. "Not what you're thinking."

He shook his head. "She was a doctor's wife. A smart girl who lived in a big house on the hill. She had my boy."

Then a thought struck.

"Rail?"

" 'Rail?' "

"Listen, tell me if you don't want me here."

" '. . . don't want me here.' "

Barry wondered whether he was keeping Rail from starting a fire, from keeping warm. Maybe Rail didn't want to be talked at and didn't want to be seen, and all the nonsense of words was keeping Rail from being a little more comfortable. Barry stood up. "I'm going on home now, Rail," he said. "Let you be alone if you want to. Just speak up now if you want me to stay."

The silence bore down. The breeze had stopped for a moment, but the clouds had started in the north. Barry moved away from the edge, out of the line of sight from the bottom of the draw. Then he sat back down.

Maybe Rail had gone back to the house after all. There'd be only John there, and maybe Nolan. Turner would be working on the ledger. No one would come out to get him if Rail were back. They'd let him sit out the whole night.

But if Rail hadn't gone back, if Rail had to sit out, within himself, then Barry knew he could, too.

He waited half an hour. Seemed like two hours. The sky kept coming down from the north. He knew that somehow there were pictures in the stars, but the only one he knew was the Dipper. He watched the clouds blow fast across it.

He stood up. There was no fire in the draw. Was Rail being cautious? Or didn't he have any matches? It occurred to him that when Rail had run off, he'd only had his jacket on, the jean one, and tennis shoes. Not even boots on. He wouldn't have had any matches.

Barry walked over to the edge once again. "Rail? I know you don't have anything, Rail. Listen, I never went away. I've been here, waiting for you to start a fire or make some sign. But it's all right to stay quiet. I'll be here."

Barry looked down the black flow of the draw. The breeze had come up stronger, and there was the scent of rain. He settled down again on the rock.

"That was fourteen years ago," Barry said. "I was twenty. Just a year older than you. Was never married to the woman, see? As soon as she knew, well, she came to me and said . . . you want to know what she said?"

The scene flashed through his mind. She had come to him in the evening in late fall. It was already dark. She had no time to wait. She was on her way from somewhere to somewhere and had to be home to the doctor. She didn't knock on the door, but rather burst in. He had been lying on the bed in his washed-out room, reading a magazine. She came across the room flying. He had thought she was going to strike him, but she stopped at the edge of the bed and looked down at him. He had not moved, except to lay the magazine on his chest.

"I'm going to have your baby," she said.

He stared. He said it aloud to Rail. "She said, 'I'm going to have your baby.' "

The words seemed to float out into the draw. The breeze destroyed any echo.

"I thought after that she would ask what I was going to do about it. I thought she would hit me. I was to blame. But she said, 'I want to leave my husband and come with you.' "

It had turned colder. The flat mesquite land was darker under the clouds. The wet smell of sage was in the air.

The rain started with a few drops. A desert storm blew quickly across the land. Barry turned his back to it. On the rim of the draw there was no protection. He thought of Rail among the trees. There was always the danger of flash flood in the draw, but below him, he knew it was wide enough that it was a simple matter to be safe. He tried to see Rail's movement.

The rain washed through quickly without thunder or lightning, leaving again the stars in its wake. Barry was soaked and cold and sat on the ledge shivering. It had lasted only ten minutes at most. The sage smell was strong and the rock glistening wet as the moon started up over the mountain.

He had said nothing to Rail during the storm, knowing that words could not have penetrated the sound of the rain. It seemed brighter now in the draw, as though the rain had lightened the canyon walls.

"She never appeared more beautiful to me than at that moment. I guess she'd resolved everything in her own mind. But I couldn't do it. Oh, at first, when she told me and said what she wanted, I was happy. But when she left to go home, I looked back at my room and at what I was, and I saw it was impossible. We didn't belong to the same world. We could never have been happy." Barry stopped. "So I know a little bit, too, about growing up and admitting to myself. You don't have to worry about anything, Rail."

Barry took out the harp again. The moon had passed the crest of the mountain and bathed the wet land. With shaking hands he put the metal to his mouth and blew on the harp the long wailing notes of his saddest song.

The buildings of the ranch spread out through the trees. On the far end, just where the trees ended, was the bunkhouse where Barry, John, Nolan, and Rail lived. Barry walked onto the porch at six-thirty.

He stood for a long moment, shivering, looking out at the sun. It burned his tired eyes.

John came out. "Find him?" John asked.

"No." Barry looked at the older man. "Didn't he come back here?"

"Not last night."

"Then he must still be down in the draw," Barry said. "I talked to him all last night."

"What'd he say?"

"Lots of things you wouldn't understand."

The two men stood in silence. Nolan came out. He was a small, ferret-like man with dark eyes and hair. He had a toothpick in his mouth.

"Where you been?" Nolan asked.

"Up on the rim of the draw," Barry said.

"Looking for Rail," John explained.

"Any luck?"

"Nope."

From across the way, Turner came out of his house into the sun. He walked toward the three of them with easy strides. Every morning he gave them their work assignments for the day. John and Nolan went out to meet him halfway.

Barry watched them standing out in the sun. He couldn't hear their voices, but he knew they were talking about the day's work. When Nolan and John had started off toward the barn, Turner came over to where Barry stood on the porch.

"How do you feel?" Turner asked.

"All right."

"Stay up there all night?"

Barry nodded.

"Just got a call," Turner said. "He's all right."

"Where is he?"

"In Aylard. The sheriff called. They've got him locked up."

"What do you mean locked up?"

"Rail was drunk last night in town. I guess he was bragging he'd put it to one of the girls. Somebody got mad. Rail's pretty feisty when he's drunk."

"Want me to go in and get him?"

Turner nodded. "I told the sheriff somebody'd be in. He said you'd need thirty dollars."

"I've got it," Barry said.

"Okay. Let me know when you get back. I'll be down in the meadow."

Turner turned away and walked across toward the barn where John and Nolan had gone. Barry stayed on the porch. Finally, he went inside to change clothes. There wasn't any hurry to get to town. Rail could wait a little longer.

The Man Who Paid to Sleep

The analyst is a severe-looking woman with her hair pulled back and Coke-bottle glasses that make her eyes seem twice as large as they should be. Her forehead has two wrinkles on it, and she nervously presses them together with her fingers. A loose smock hides the body. I sit opposite her in a leather chair. Plush. It's always plush in these offices of doctors.

"Do I have to talk to that?" I ask, pointing to the tape recorder she has running on the table between us.

"For posterity," she says. "And so I can review your case."

"If I stick."

"It's confidential."

I nod. It's all confidential, everything, but they have you pegged in some office someplace. The government has you numbered, the banks, the insurance companies. "Sounds like a zoo."

I wonder what the analyst really looks like under the disguise. I imagine the TV ad transformation of the tough-looking businesswoman into the siren. Remove the glasses, restyle the hiar, lay in eye shadow and lipstick, tighten up the clothes, throw away the two-pound shoes . . .

"Well, Mr. Ashe, what are we here for?" she asks.

"You're here to make money."

"I'm here to help you."

"At fifty bucks a throw."

She smiles. When she smiles her face breaks to pieces, like shattering glass. It's not a good smile. The teeth don't come out, and it never really comes alive.

"The fee only makes you work that much more. It's incentive. If it didn't hurt you a little, you wouldn't try so hard."

"Bullshit," I mean to say, but actually it comes out, "I'd try anything. I want to sleep."

"Sleep?"

The word excites me. I must admit this analyst has a smooth voice. She says sleep, even in a question, as though she's one of those beautiful, full-bodied women that the magazines are always throwing at you.

"It's been weeks," I say, "since I've had a reasonable sleep."

"You seem alert and in good condition."

"The regular doctor says I'm fit enough for the army."

"What do you mean 'reasonable sleep'?"

"More than three hours. I'm lucky if I get three hours." I look at her. "What are you writing down?"

"Notes."

"Notes on me?"

"To refresh my memory."

These people are always trying to get you down. Either that or they can't remember their own names and addresses. I understand it completely. It's their job.

"I don't want to go into the army."

"Have you done your service?"

"Yes. Oh, yes. I was a missionary."

"You don't strike me as the missionary type."

"I was in the Air Force. Valdosta, Georgia. A fine place if you like to sweat. I was a desk man."

"When did you first notice that you were not sleeping?"

"When I woke up."

"I mean, Mr. Ashe, when did you notice you were not sleeping on a regular basis?"

She doesn't like sarcasm, I can see. "I figured after a while it had to be in the brain."

"It might be," she says. "But let me build up a little history."

"About two months ago."

She writes.

"About two months ago I started waking up almost as soon as I'd go to bed. You know I was always one of those lucky people who can sleep anywhere and anytime. All I needed was a pillow and my eyes closed. Sometimes not even a pillow. But I began to wake up and not go back to sleep again. I couldn't figure it out."

"Did you try anything?"

"I tried lots of things. Sominex, Sleep-EZ, booze. I tried vacations and exercise. Even ritual. I would watch the late news, read a half-hour, drink a cup of warm milk. It became an obsession. I'd turn down the covers at a certain angle, take off my left shoe first, put my clothes backwards on a hanger in the closet. When that failed, I would adjust. I figured it was like setting the timing on a car. By trial and error I was bound to find the right combination."

"But you didn't."

"It was worse. I'd spend nights in turmoil, wondering where I'd gone wrong. My work suffered. I mean, my business suffered. I do travel. Arrange destinations, book flights, you know. But I started getting irritable at work. I'd chew erasers, shuffle papers around. I couldn't tolerate mistakes. Yell at customers."

"And now?"

"I got out."

"You're not working?"

"I own it. I got a manager."

"And sleep?"

There's the voice again. "Off and on. Exhaustion consumes me at different times. I never know when. Sometimes hanging on a bus strap. Sometimes at a basketball game. Once I put my face down into my food at a restaurant. What kind of life is that?"

The analyst looks at my face—a Scandinavian face, not bad. My features are compressed a little toward the nose. Gray eyes, electric hair, wide lips. I've got a facial tic now that I never had before: my eyes jerk back involuntarily into my skull.

"What about prescriptions?"

"They worked for a while until I was doing doubles and triples. I was screaming at inanimate objects, throwing pillows across the room . . ."

The analyst sits back. "There are cases in medical history of human beings going six or eight weeks without sleep. Beethoven stayed up for days working on his symphonies. Edison . . ."

"I'm a travel agent."

"Tell me a little of your past."

"My mother didn't let me have a night light."

"Fifty dollars an hour, Mr. Ashe."

I sober up, a schoolboy scolded by his teacher. I say, "A's in history, D's in math. I played B-team basketball and ran a fair mile. My first sexual encounter was at fifteen with a girl a year older."

"What girl?"

"Courtney Martin."

She writes that down. I see we have touched her subject.

"What were your feelings about Courtney Martin?"

I shrug. "Fine."

"I mean, how did you react?"

"Quickly. It was my first time." I smile, looking at her.

"I'm not asking what happened, but rather what your emotions were."

"No guilt."

"None?"

"I never met a woman I didn't like."

"Now we're getting somewhere."

"At least until now."

"Keep going."

"Why don't you do something about your appearance? Get a little flair?"

"Appearance bothers you?"

"It bothers me at these prices."

"I thought you cared about sleeping."

"I do, but I don't want to dream about you."

"Why should that matter?"

"Because you could do better."

"Judged in whose terms?"

"Mine."

"Mr. Ashe, we're trying to get beyond the appearances of things. You don't care about the appearance of sleep, do you?"

She has me there. I thought I would get her going, but I can tell she lacks imagination. "No."

"Tell me about Courtney Martin."

To tell the truth, I have not thought about Courtney Martin in years, though I feel she has always been in my mind somewhere. It's like learning two plus two early in life and afterwards having that knowledge when you're figuring your income tax. I wonder where and when I learned two plus two.

The analyst eyes me for catching up on my memory.

"We went to different schools," I say, as though that explains it. "We didn't know each other well."

I can see the analyst wants me to continue, but I pause again, thinking how there always was a certain sinister freedom in not having my friends in on the details of Courtney Martin. Courtney was my secret, and I suddenly realize I have never told anyone else about her. No one. "I don't want to talk about Courtney Martin," I answer. "She couldn't have anything to do with my not sleeping."

The analyst leans over and snaps off the recorder. "Mr. Ashe, anything and everything may have a bearing on the matter."

"Maybe," I say, "but I'm not telling you about her."

We go on to other shards in the sandpile of the past: how my mother locked me in a closet for a day and lost the key, how my father threw me into the middle of a lake to teach me to swim. Little things that warped me good. But all the time I am thinking about Courtney Martin.

When it's over the analyst says, "Next time we'll talk about your feelings for this girl."

"What girl?"

"You think about it."

"Do you promise to spruce up?"

The analyst smiles, cracking her face up like a piece of wadded paper.

Out on the street I try to get the feel of the world again. It's as though I have been in a sauna in the analyst's office and out here there is wind and air and the noise of human life. I figure out what street I'm on, but I really have no direction. I don't feel the least bit tired, but somehow my energy is not so frenetic as usual, and I walk slowly for a couple of blocks.

How can I help thinking about Courtney Martin? The analyst has put me on the trail.

Courtney's parents and my parents sometimes played mixed doubles at the public park. Courtney and I would hang around and talk and listen to them scream at each other. Maybe we'd hit a few if there was an open court. Neither of us was any good. She was thin then, with barely a figure, and I used to laugh at the way she would whack the shit out of the ball with a big groan.

"What's so funny?" she'd ask indignantly when the ball would skip by me. "You didn't get it."

"I will someday," I would say.

And she would turn without deigning to answer and walk back to the baseline to start another rally.

One day our parents were making fools of themselves over a line call, and in the heat of the argument my father walked off with her father's racquet, or vice versa. When the mistake was discovered, I was assigned to make the exchange.

I remember driving across town on my Mo-ped. It was one of those forever sky days with blue and green trees and high, lazy white clouds. It was a fitting day for almost anything except being yelled at by Mr. Martin about my father's eyesight. But I was spared.

When Courtney answered the door there was an electric charge in the air, a static that no amount of laundry spray could have neutralized. I knew her parents were not home. She looked beautiful. She had on white shorts and a blue blouse, and there was a thin line of sweat on her upper lip. Nothing could have matched her then in my eyes. The sun had given her freckles, and her eyes seemed bluer against the dark skin of her face. Her hair was smooth blond, falling to her shoulders, and as I stepped inside I asked myself: *should this be?*

How many years ago was that? I count up: twelve. Courtney, wherever she is, is twenty-eight.

I walk five blocks without being aware that I walk without regard to traffic lights or cars. I am trying to remember every detail of that one afternoon of my life.

There is really nothing romantic about it. No soft lights, no music. It was a dumpy house; they were always talking about moving. On her dressing table were two pictures of other boys beside her own school picture, which looked about as much like the Courtney that came to the door as King Kong looks like Catherine Deneuve. The room was pink and littered with lace and insignia from a foreign school. We both felt the constant dread that her mother would walk in any moment and call out, "Courtney?" in the voice she always used on the tennis court.

Maybe it was all those wrong things that made it right. I felt like a spy in an enemy camp, putting one over on the home team, as it were. How could I have possibly felt any guilt? Nothing bad happened.

I duck into a phone booth and call the analyst to tell her it's none of her business what I think about Courtney Martin. The receptionist says she's with another patient.

"Tell her Mr. Ashe is going to shoot himself."

I wait half a minute and the analyst comes on.

"What is it?" she asks.

I like the voice. Cool, like water. "I've decided for the ultimate sleep," I say.

"Where are you?"

"In a phone booth on Penny Lane."

"Did you interrupt me as a joke?"

"I wanted to ask you what shade of lipstick you prefer."

She hangs up.

I smile, feeling good.

In the afternoon I go up to my apartment to try to sleep, but nothing happens. I lie on the bed with my eyes open, watching sun patterns dance on the ceiling. Always Courtney is there like two plus two.

Despite the brief encounter, or perhaps because of it, we did not keep close. Her father finally moved out of that dump to another town. We never even wrote.

How can I describe the sensation of making love to her? We were children. It was over in twenty seconds. Yet there was something about those twenty seconds that now seems as eternal as art. What? Her legs were skinny. I liked her breasts but they weren't very big. She kissed well. Then I remember how she used to hit the ball on the tennis court.

I get up, go to the phone, hardly knowing where to start. I've forgotten her father's first name. I dial information.

"For what city?"

"Colorado Springs."

"Go ahead."

"Martin."

The operator has some kind of chipmunk's voice. "I'm sorry . . ."

"How many Martins are there?"

"I can give you three at a time."

I hang up. I call her high school, which gives me her college in California. They give me some address in New York. I call information but she has no phone. I hang up. She's probably married and has children.

I stand around a moment, then sigh and curse. I'm wasting time.

I pack a suitcase hurriedly, not bothering to ask myself why since I don't need a motel. I call a friend at United Airlines who gets me on the next flight to New York.

I'm light as I drift up over the clouds and the prairies toward New York. There have been other girls. Women have been one of the life forces, like fire or rain. The travel business is glamorous; I get along as well as I can.

When my sleeplessness began I called some friends to help me, and for a while it worked as well as the prescriptions. Maikke James was a Dutch girl who married an American who later claimed he was impotent. If he was, she had made him that way by uncanny lovemaking that could squeeze you dry. Pamela Pierson was slower and subtler, but equally voracious. She was deceptively nymphlike but had the heart of a whore. She insisted upon three orgasms as part of the deal, and she left me more unconscious than asleep. And Irma Jacobs—a girl with a body and a soul so attuned to pleasure that sex must have been her true religion. She babbled and chanted and writhed without a shred of inhibition, and more than once I had to assure worried neighbors that there were no murders in progress in my apartment.

But even the daze in which these girls left me began to be intolerable. There is a moment at the end of lovemaking when you either turn away into oblivion or you lie awake forever, and more and more I began to miss the turn and continue on into the stark blank realm of questioning what I was doing and why. In the mornings I was left deaf, dumb, and blind, and somehow had to explain to the girls that I was beyond hope.

We circle New York, and I see the Empire State Building and the whole bit. I wonder what I expect to accomplish, even if I find her.

Come to think of it, I did get one letter from Courtney. It was a couple of years later, written on the anniversary of the day, and it came from someplace strange like Carlsbad Caverns or Mount Rushmore. As I recall, it was inappropriately newsy. She was with her parents and it was a bore; she was doing all right in school; how was I? That sort of thing. But there was one confusing line that I am trying to piece together. Something about infinity and expecting a break in the weather, or about getting a break in the weather and finding . . . I can't remember it exactly.

The first thing I do is rent a car and take my life into my own hands. I've been ninety-two hours without sleep, and I know it can come at any moment, like in death against a bridge abutment. I ask directions and within minutes of leaving the airport I am thoroughly lost. If I drive far enough I will get somewhere.

Hours later I conclude that Courtney Martin does not exist. No one at her address has ever heard of her. She must have joined a space culture, I decide, as I drive down Fifth Avenue.

Even in the short space of ten minutes, before the driver behind me finally shakes loose the door of the rental car, I dream. I am floating on an air mattress in the ocean with two-thirds of the world's creatures beneath me. My eyes are open and I see beyond the sky, which appears blue, to some distant planet. The beings on this planet aim a gun at me and pull the trigger, but they are so far away that I see the bullet coming in slow motion, taking its sweet time. My analyst's face suddenly appears on the head of the bullet—her thick glasses and the smile that crackles her skin like a weatherbeaten Cheshire cat. As she floats through space she removes the glasses and her eyes appear like whirling nebulae. Somewhere in my body there is a convulsive spasm as I realize she is eager to make contact. I watch her, half forgetting there is a bullet behind her face, thinking there is always enough time to roll over into the sea.

The man who has shaken the door off is unkind, screaming, "What kind of idiot are you? Asleep? My brother's a cop. I'll get you thrown into the hoosegow."

"The hoosegow?" I ask incredulously. I laugh and cannot stop, doubled over the steering wheel until he punches me in the ear.

I cruise out to Coney Island and watch the people for an hour. It's a grim picture, these New Yorkers jammed up on the polluted oceanside, the sun baking them like pot pies. Do I really expect to find Courtney Martin here?

I probe further. Who is the person who keeps track of you throughout your life if you have no parents? Two answers: God, who is indisposed, and your college roommate.

The school refuses to divulge the name of Courtney Martin's roommate over the telephone. So I fly to California to shake it out of them.

The roommate is Marcella Penn from Oceanside. I make a few more calls. Marcella is married and has moved to Long Beach. Marcella is not home. I rent another car. I've never been a sightseer, so while I'm waiting for Marcella to get home, I drive over to Long Beach to wait on her doorstep. Her husband, Ivan, a bruiser, arrives before she does, and he wants to know what I'm doing there. I explain the story about Courtney, and he says, "Oh, that dame."

"Where is she?" If I had one, I would hold my hat in my hand.

"New York."

"She's not in New York," I say.

"What do you want to find her for? She'll only cause you trouble."

"Just a lark." My nerves are running a string of fireworks.

"You want a beer?"

I have a beer and we talk about how he was cut by the Rams. After a while he asks, "How long did you say it had been?"

"Twelve years."

He nods and smiles out of one corner of his mouth. I let it slide. I don't want anyone to say anything that will change my image. I don't want to know anything about her before I see her.

Marcella arrives, dressed in shorts and halter, with a chocolate-faced child holding her kneecap. I make it brief. She gives me an address in Beverly Hills.

I drive over on the freeway. My mind is in reverie, as though each neuron of the brain were a diamond on a lake full of sun. In this state I can go forever. Sea, sky, road, car: they make no difference to me.

That day twelve years ago flashes in and out of my consciousness like a strobe light's illumination of a discotheque. I see Courtney's calm face, her eyes closed, as though she is in some trance. Only once she bites her lower lip so I know she is alive. I see myself confused, awkward, not certain of the point of impact. I look around to see whether anyone is watching. Every creak of the house makes me jump. Then I see the youthful bodies joined somehow for an instant, and I smile like a dolt.

On the outskirts of Beverly Hills I take a room. I need someplace anonymous in case things develop. I get a shower, experience time lag. While I am drying myself and contemplating events, I pick up the phone and dial my analyst.

Should I do it?" I ask.

"By all means," she says. "What?"

"Call Courtney Martin."

"Where are you, Mr. Ashe."

"Holiday Inn."

"You sound far away."

"Beverly Hills. I'm buying you some spring fashions."

"What is this all about?"

"Courtney Martin lives here."

I imagine the analyst's impatient face, her gesture of pressing the wrinkles of her forehead together with her fingers. The silence suggests she is trying to remember who I am.

"The man who is paying to sleep, right?"

"Mr. Ashe, your next visit is scheduled for a week from now."

"I wanted to ask you about this dream I had."

She gives in. I hear her sigh.

I tell her the dream about the bullet, making sure I describe her glasses and her smile. Someone needs to shake her up. I leave off with the bullet poised only a few feet from my heart.

"What happens then?"

"I don't know."

She pauses. "And now you've tracked down Courtney Martin?"

"I'm right on her doorstep."

"Have you slept to have this dream?"

"Ten minutes at a red light in New York."

"Mr. Ashe, I think you ought to get back here as quickly as possible."

"And give up Courtney?" The suggestion is so ludicrous that I do not consider it.

"Your state of mind is such that . . ."

"I'll bring you some skin cream," I say, and hang up.

I start to dial Courtney Martin, but then decide I would rather see her. The moment of first contact and all that. I dress and check myself out in the mirror. Surprisingly, sleeplessness has left few marks on me. The eyes seem bleached, and I have lost some weight. Will she still recognize me?

Being lost in strange places is becoming familiar. I ask directions four times, trying to find Rodeo Drive.

Finally there it is. I cruise slowly, letting the raw power of nerves take its toll. I try to figure out my first words to her, but I keep getting flashes of bare skin and freckles which make heat come to my face.

"Courtney?" I jump, nearly running head-on into a tour bus. If her mother had come in that day, I probably would have done nothing but roll over onto my back like they do in the movies and say hi. Twenty seconds. Jesus Christ. Twenty seconds twelve years ago.

I find the number. Park the car. It's a nice house with no name on the mailbox. I mean a *nice* house, maybe six or seven bedrooms. The garage doors are open. Three of them. The spaces are empty. She's not home.

I knock anyway. Wait. Knock again. I hear footsteps. A maid opens the door.

"Is Courtney here?"

"She's at the club," the maid says, not offering more.

I desperately want to ask questions: Is she married? What does she do? Is there a photograph of her? But I renege. After debating how I can wait gracefully, I ask how I can get to the club.

The club is huge, bigger than the public park I remember. There is a soft blue-green glow to things, not quite real. I sit for a moment in my car trying to stay awake. A terrible fatigue has suddenly hit me. The club mansion wavers, the shiny cars stacked in the sun hurt my eyes.

I stagger out. The fresh air is tepid, sliding over me like oil. I make my way inside to the desk and ask for Courtney Martin.

The man stares at me for a moment. "Who?"

"Courtney Martin."

He draws a blank. "No one . . . oh, you mean Courtney Mauritania."

I make some feeble gesture of assent.

"She's playing tennis." He motions for me to pass through glass doors beyond his arm. "Right through there."

I go. Courtney Mauritania? I wander down a manicured path, the sound of tennis balls being hit becoming more and more audible. My pace quickens. The path opens out into a field where white-clad figures run back and forth under a whirling blue sky.

As I approach I slow down. My metabolism seems to have stopped entirely. Legs heavy, eyes barely open. I walk stealthily to the fence and look through.

I pass quickly over the ones who are obviously not Courtney. I know what to expect. I feel my insides consumed by hunger, my head spins. There she is, just as I have pictured her.

She's on Court 2, hitting with the club pro. I whistle softly through my teeth. I watch her bring the racquet back, step in. Uhh. It's Courtney.

She's beautiful. There's no other word. Her legs are long and slender, her breasts seem tight even when she strokes the ball. Her hair is tied back, long, and I imagine how it must look loose upon a pillow. Uhh. She cracks the ball hard. Though it's difficult to see her face because she is constantly moving, I can tell it's perfect. Perfect. Uhh. She doesn't miss.

I close my eyes, drift a little way into sleep, and then return. I watch her hit and hit. She's good. She sends back every shot to the baseline, and even Robert Redford, the pro, has trouble getting them back. At the net she's quick. She volleys decisively. Uhh.

After half an hour I'm barely able to keep standing. I roll along the fence, holding the wire with my hands to keep upright. My effort is valiant, and I last until she quits and puts a cover on her racquet. She walks across Court 1, looks at me hanging there, and goes into the pro shop.

Courtney Mauritania? I feel embarrassed, lost. She comes out of the shop, takes her hair down and shakes it out. Amazing. Then she walks along the path close to me. She looks at me again, says hello, starts to go by, then stops.

I struggle to keep my eyes open.

She says, "You look familiar."

I nod. Her face is dark from the sun and the eyes are bluer than any others I have ever seen.

She takes two steps toward me, looks at me closely, barely five feet away. I keep imagining skinny legs and her biting her lip.

Then she shrugs and says, "I guess not."

I sleep for three hours leaning against the fence. A club guard finally wakes me and throws me out. I sleep another four hours in the parking lot with the car door open. Another guard thinks I'm dead. He calls a cab, and I sleep all the way to the airport. I sleep through the flight home. The stewardess wakes me.

"Should I call someone, sir? Are you all right?"

I give her my analyst's number, and I sleep at the airport terminal until she arrives.

It's about time.

Incident in the High Country

They had followed the creek bed for a mile through deep snow and then had cut up the left slope through the trees to catch the ridge at about the middle. They worked their way up on their touring skis, Leland breaking the trail, followed by Hildy and McKay. After an hour they came out of the trees and climbed to the ridge. The road had disappeared behind them, and there was no sound of cars moving up or down the pass.

"There it is," Leland said, shaking the snow from his skis and pointing ahead. "That's home for a few days."

Tucked off the wind line of a hill was a board A-frame, and McKay felt a sense of wonder descend over him. He wondered not at the hut itself, but that it was there, so high up in the immensity of that land. For beyond the hut lay the contours of the high country, the white barren snow hills above timberline, one after another leading up to the rim of the Divide, and distinguished only by height and shadow and distance.

Leland was a blond, thin-lipped boy, who at twenty-three had far more experience in the mountains than McKay. Hildy was wild about him. She would go on these tangents with certain boys—mountaineers usually—and go off with them for months at a time. She was an enthusiastic skier and never at a loss for something to do. That was why McKay had called her. Hildy was his cousin, and he'd always felt close to her. Sometimes when he was down he would go over and let her cheerful manner bring him out. And so with that new terrible feeling he had, when he could not stand his own thoughts any longer, he had telephoned and she had invited him along to the high country for the weekend.

They crossed along the ridge, stroking evenly with legs and arms. Higher up still, just short of the hut, they stopped again to rest. They were above the trees and the world was a bright white, and the sky stretched wide and clear the length of the valley behind them.

"The biggest bowl is behind the rise there," Leland said, pointing right. "Wait until you see it!"

McKay could wait. He was tired from the climb and wanted to get to the hut. He felt a little uneasy with such a stark land around him. It was so immaculate and impenetrable in the winter, and he was not sure he should have come at all.

Suddenly Hildy lifted her ski pole. "Somebody's up there."

McKay strained his eyes against the glare and saw she was right. Far away against the white of the mountain a red speck edged across one of the hills.

"Looks as though he's on snowshoes and heading up to the bowl," Leland said matter-of-factly.

"Is he alone?" That was all that interested McKay.

"Shouldn't be."

But they could see no one else. They watched for a few minutes as the red point of color slowly traversed the huge field of snow. No one else followed.

The hut was in the drifts and they had to dig their way in. Then, while Leland got water from the the stream, McKay built the fire. Hildy unpacked the food from the backpacks.

"What do you think of all this?" she asked.

"I hope Leland doesn't mind my coming along."

"I explained as much as I could to him. Everybody gets down once in a while."

He had come along because he had been driven to it by the sheer weight of things he could not face anymore. He had told himself these things were little bits of life that everyone had to face, but the commonality was no solace. Those small things seemed to hang upon him like invisible pieces of iron, each adding to the weight of the whole, accumulating by seconds and by minutes of each day until the weight of it had become too much. At first he had tried to understand it, to resolve and to break away to something new, but each time he decided upon a new direction, he found a new difficulty of living. With each movement the weight simply became greater and all his beliefs changed; he did not know where to turn. His life had become too full of shortcomings.

"I don't know what to think about the country," McKay said.

"It's just good to get away. You won't find anyone else here, and you can do what you need to, to sort things out."

"There was that one on the hill," McKay said.

Leland came in with the water. The small room was already beginning to heat up.

"You won't see him again," Hildy said.

"Who?" Leland asked, taking off his coat.

"The one on the hill this afternoon."

Leland shook his head and looked to McKay. "He's probably gone cross-country over the Divide."

The thought of it frightened McKay. Just the idea of being alone in that high country, with the cold and the night coming, worried him. He wondered what it was one had to have to be able to do such a thing.

And in the night, with Leland and Hildy asleep in sleeping bags on the wide mattress beside him, McKay woke up. The fire had gone out in the stove and the silence of the room disturbed him. He was used to traffic outside his window, to the sounds of sirens and trucks unloading and city repair.

He sat up. The moon caught a line in the cracked glass in the window and he leaned forward to look out. Across the stream was a cliff with a jutting cornice of ice, and below it the white valley flowed away into the darkness. He felt as though he were gazing upon some beautiful and unknown soil, a place unearthly, which would always haunt him like his very best dreams.

For McKay was thirty years old, just beyond the possibility of going back and believing in something new. He understood that the ages between twenty and thirty were the hardest to live, but he had moved very quickly through that time before he had realized what was happening to him. He knew that his lean looks had changed in ten years and that he was rounder of face. Yet he had retained somehow a certain expression of innocence, capable of deception. But he was not capable of deceiving himself, and at last he had seen that all one's hopes and thoughts must be revised to include the body and the relentless pressure of time. Looking past thirty was suddenly like seeing one's first true vision of death.

The next day they awoke early. The sun had slanted in across the mountains to the east, and the sky was the light blue of ice. Leland was the first up to make the fire, and then, while Hildy made breakfast, the two men waxed the skis for the day's climb. Toward ten, with small nylon day packs filled with lunch, they left the hut for the Divide.

McKay had never been in the high country in winter. He had toured in ski areas and had done downhill, but he had never been up where the land was open and endless and without a track.

They climbed slowly, Leland breaking trail as on the previous day, and it took them all morning to climb two long rising hills of snow. McKay kept up because he climbed on the packed snow of the others, but each time he reached the top of a ridge, he believed he was there. And always these were false ridges, and beyond was another, gently rising up toward the Divide.

"Any sign of our friend?" McKay asked.

"He must have gone over and down the back."

"Not even tracks?"

"Maybe we'll hit them," Leland said, "if the wind hasn't blown them clean."

By early afternoon they had crossed the snowshoe tracks and Leland followed them on the traverse. He seemed never to tire and to love what he was doing. McKay watched his expression with envy. It was an expression he wished for himself—to find and to love what he did.

Near the top Leland cut back from the snowshoe tracks and took the last part on his own. He struggled up, lifting the heavy snow forward with each step. But he did not rest.

At the top they stood for a few minutes on that edge, where in summer the melting snow would flow into two separate oceans. McKay had never seen so many mountains.

"Weather's coming," Leland said, pointing off to the clouds in the northwest. "Let's ski to the bowl and then head back."

McKay wanted to rest there and wait. He was tired from the physical work, and the view was unending. "I'll follow the tracks back," he said.

But at last Hildy convinced him to come. "It'll be easy down," she said.

McKay followed. He angled his skis downward and let himself fall through the deep powder. It was a good feeling, that gliding, and he let himself sink as though into sleep. Snow was everywhere and there was nothing to watch for and he closed his eyes.

Then, ahead of him Leland stopped and began climbing up again to his left. Hildy was close behind Leland; McKay trudged up again to where they stood. Then he was there, too, looking down into the bowl.

It was a huge scoop out of the mountain, and the sides of it curved down sharply from the Divide. Across the bowl was the cliff McKay had seen the night before from the window. But now it did not look like part of a beautiful and foreign world. It cut up in a dark swath of rock to the ice cornice which hung out over the edge.

"I guess your friend made it," Leland said.

For along that highest ridge at the top of the bowl, the red figure had emerged from behind a crest of snow.

"Must have spent the night up there," Leland said.

McKay barely heard. He was watching the solitary figure of the man move out along the ridge, closer to the cornice of ice. He was in clear sight now, and McKay could see his blue pants and his red parka, bright in the sun. It was as if he were watching someone in a dream of his own—a nightmare he had had a thousand times, and he was in awe and reverence for that man.

Leland and Hildy moved on, skiing down to the bottom of the millions of tons of snow in the bowl. McKay forced himself to wait.

For a few precious moments he watched the top of the cliff. At last, when the others stopped, he went down.

"Do you think he sees us?" Hildy asked. She waved her ski pole in an arc over her head.

"Doesn't see us," Leland answered.

The red figure moved out onto the cornice.

McKay knew differently. Leland may have had more experience than he in the mountains, and the figure made no response to Hildy's sign, but McKay knew more about that man. In that figure on the ridge were McKay's own nightmares, and he knew the man saw them. From that height the man could see the vastness of the mountains and the whole width of the sky and the great white apron of snow below him. The man moved out closer to the edge of the cornice and stopped.

"He knows," McKay said. "He might not have expected to see us, but he knows we're here."

The three of them held their positions on the hill. It was cold in that altitude to stand and wait, and yet it was not possible to look away. All of them knew how brittle those cornices were, how they broke in the spring when the snow turned heavy, and how the weight upon them could snap tons of ice like a twig. McKay knew the man up there knew it, too, just as he must have known the nightmare of living.

He must have known the terrible fatigue of nights in the mountains, sleeping in snow caves and waiting, eyes opened, for the dawn. He must have known it all to fight for survival in order to reach that cornice where he inched forward with such desperation.

"He's going to fall!" Hildy said suddenly, breaking the silence.

But the man did not fall. He edged out slowly and then stopped again. For a long moment he stood, and then with wild awkward movements, like a sprinter's starting, he took two steps and jumped into that void of rocks below him, striking twice and making no sound.

McKay did not hear Hildy's scream, nor Leland's cogent explanation. He did not see their open-mouthed stares, though he looked into their faces as he passed. In that same moment that the red figure jumped, McKay was moving forward on his skis with quick strides, cutting down through the fresh snow into the bowl.

He felt himself bog down on the flat bottom of the bowl, sinking in on the narrow skis. A sweat arose immediately, but he struggled forward, flailing with arms and legs. That gulf of snow from one side of the bowl to the other seemed endless. But he tried to run.

He had to run, but it was not possible. The snow bunched up against his shins, his skis deep under the snow. He had to lift the weight of the snow with every step. He thought of traffic lights, red, blinking, but there were no traffic lights in the high country. There were no cars, nor roads, nor signs. Only space, and still he could not run.

His breath came hard and painfully in the thin air. Behind him he could hear the swish of Leland's polished technique and Hildy's voice in the distance as she called "Wait!" after them.

A small blister burned his heel, and he imagined it growing and turning red. With each stroke of the pole, with each short slide and each lift, that blister grew until it had consumed his whole foot. His whole foot pained him and the pain kept moving up his leg, and farther until the pain had engulfed his whole body. Each step across the wide field was a torture, and when he heard Leland come up close behind him, he felt an overwhelming hatred. He was helpless. He could hear Leland's breath lighter than his own, and in his disjointed vision, McKay saw the younger man's graceful stride across the track which he, McKay, had already pressed down.

And so, when Leland stepped out to run ahead, McKay swung out viciously with his pole and knocked Leland off balance into the snow.

"Hey! You crazy?"

McKay went on. That blister was burning in his brain now, and his lungs ached. He felt as though his brain and his lungs would explode him into nothingness on that great plain of snow. But he kept moving.

The cliff was approaching now, towering above him and coming faster overhead as he neared it. He looked over his shoulder and saw Hildy helping Leland out of the powder. They were all in the shadow of the cliff now, and the line of the shadow was rising against the run on the hill where they had stood and watched.

He found a patch of the red jacket, an arm protruding from the snow, like a drowning man reaching up to grasp with his hand the last bit of air. There was blood on the snow and a deep pocket where the weight of the body had fallen in. McKay tried to brace himself in the loose snow, but he sank down as he pulled.

Leland and Hildy came up. "Are you crazy?" Leland asked. "Hildy said you were crazy."

McKay looked at him with a glare. "Help me get him out," he ordered.

Leland came around and helped pull. They brought the red jacket out. It was ripped where the body had hit the rocks and the blood still flowed.

They brought his head out.

"He wasn't dead," McKay said. "He wasn't dead when he hit."

The man's mouth was filled with the snow he had sucked in beneath the surface. It had turned to ice, and with a rough motion, McKay scraped the man's mouth clean with his fingers.

"Doesn't matter now," Leland said.

"He suffocated before I could get to him."

"Hit his head and was probably dead already."

McKay felt his anger rise. He didn't like the way Leland kept breaking off the beginnings of sentences.

"We've got to get him down," McKay said.

Blood still oozed from the man's temple toward the open eyes.

"Going to have to get down ourselves," Leland said, pointing to the clouds coming quickly in over the Divide.

"Then you go ahead," McKay told him. "I'm going to bring him down."

Leland stood and cleared his goggles meticulously and strapped them on. "We just don't have time now," Leland said. "Maybe you don't know what it's like up here when it snows."

"He doesn't know," Hildy put in.

"Won't be able to get him down," Leland said. "Not if you can't see."

McKay looked from Leland to Hildy. "Think it's foolish, huh? Think I'm crazy."

"We know where he is," Hildy said, as evenly as she could. "We'll come back."

Across the bowl toward the low hill the sky was still blue, but as they stood waiting, the clouds sank and the ridge was enveloped in snow sifting down.

"You go ahead," McKay said.

The wind started harder.

"What's the point of it? What for?" Hildy asked.

McKay was silent. He looked down at the blood in the snow and at the eyes which still held a brilliance in the dull light. That man did not have to tell the living anything. He didn't have to tell anyone what was inside him, and neither did McKay.

Leland turned. The snow had started to fall. "Come on, Hildy," he said, moving his skis around and taking her arm.

"Wait." Hildy pulled away from him and went close to McKay.

"Nobody's here," she said, speaking quickly. "That dead man isn't anybody at all. You never knew him. You never met him when he was alive. You don't know what he was, who he was, or why he killed himself. He's not a human being now. But there will be two bodies here if you try to bring him down."

McKay looked at her. He had never felt so exhausted. "You don't know that."

"It's certain," Leland said.

"*You* don't know that either."

Then Hildy turned, too, and Leland led the way, poling and gliding. McKay could hear the swishing sound for only a few seconds in the wind. He did not look up.

He went right to work and tied the hands of the body together. He got loose the battered snowshoes and raised the weight of the body onto his back, so that the hands fell around his neck. The body was heavier than he had thought it would be, and hard to balance.

As soon as he could, he began moving, holding tightly to a leg with one hand and using only one pole to keep himself up. He could not lift and glide even in the empty tracks of Leland and Hildy. But that blister he had felt before had now disappeared.

The snow came. In the gray of the dusk the snow was invisible, but he could feel it pricking his face as it blew across through the bowl. He carried on in the blizzard that followed, too, moving foward with even slower steps. The open snow made him blind, and the earth seemed a mass of that one grey—not cold, but simply a uniformity which dissolved shape and distance and time.

As best he could he made his way in the others' tracks, and then even the feeling of the hard surface was gone. The snow had covered the tracks over or he had lost them. The wind came across still, with nothing to stop it.

Finally in the full darkness he stopped. He could feel he was off the windline because he had suddenly dropped over a drift into a slight depression in the snow. The wind lessened, and there he put the man down.

With his skis he packed down as much snow as he could, and then he took one ski off. Standing on the packed snow, he dug down with the ski. Working quickly, he dug a deep pit, and then standing in the pit he dug sideways into the snow, hollowing out a place to lie. He moved the man's body down into the shelter.

McKay knew he would survive that night. He had survived all the other nights, and he could live through one more. The others would be wrong. And McKay climbed into the burrow, too, out of the wind and the snow, and, inching up close, he put his arms around the dead man.

The Mad Artist's Dream of Hues

"It's too cold," I say, pointing to the window around which cracks appear like scars on the Victorian wallpaper. "I need to be able to stand there."

The plasterer nods as though he understands and puts down the materials he has brought in. He lifts his hand and feels the draft, and I see his fingernails etched in white moving over the space. His hands are speckled from his last job and look older than his face. His face shows superficiality, not about his work, but about something in his life. I guess his age to be twenty-eight, four years younger than mine. His eyes give him away, the transparent blue of sky, though without the depth. He had taken his time shaving, the skin of his face smooth and the sideburns immaculately cut, like edging in a garden. He looks solid, as though he would be a good and obedient soldier. I wonder whether he had ever thought anything through.

He goes out and returns with a ladder, which he props against the wall.

"It shouldn't take long. Is this the only window?"

"This is the only one which has the view."

He lays a cloth and begins to chisel out the old plaster from around the window. He works well, at least while I am there, and I think of having him fix other things around the house that Richard never gets to. Then I remember it is only a rented house.

"Do things happen?" the plasterer asks.

"Sorry?"

"Out the window here. Does anything go on?"

I nod and look past him. It does not look like much now: a blank wall of leafless trees, the sky quilted blue in the angles of the close branches. The past few days have been cold and rainy, taking the last of the leaves. Beyond the close trees is the heavy undergrowth, cleared slightly, where the backyard expands borderless into the woods.

"What things?" he asks.

"Well . . ." I try to avoid being impolite, but do not want to answer. It is not his business to know what goes on here, and I think to myself, remembering

the day the goshawk struck through the just-green trees last spring I had come in from a walk and was taking off my jacket when the bird knifed down and grasped the wire top of one of Richard's rat cages that he kept there on the porch The hawk had come in so swiftly and cleanly that for a moment I wondered whether it was really so close to the house and the window But it caught its talon in the wire and for the instant that it took to extricate itself its reality was upon me, the brilliant white and black and gray head the spread of the barred tail and the fanatical red eye.

The plasterer does not seem to mind my not answering, and he goes about mixing the new plaster with water brought from the bathroom sink. This room is mine, my studio that Richard had promised me in order to get me to move with him from the city two years ago. It is a wing of the house with a separate entrance, an ideal place, and I cannot explain why I cannot work here. I have filled the space with canvasses, easels, but in two years I have not been able to finish anything.

I sense without being certain that the plasterer is watching me, and I turn away from the window. He is mixing the plaster back and forth with a spatula, scraping the sides of the pail. I like the sound.

While I was not looking he has put on a small hat which does not begin to cover the length of his hair. The hat confines his face so that his features seem compressed, and I am conscious that his face had a missing element, like a sketch without the critical lines. He smiles disarmingly, as though innocent of everything except a lack of concentration. I am aware for the first time that we are alone.

He goes back to work, as though his smile has meant nothing.

I turn away again and console myself at the window, thinking back

to the day the neighbor's son whose name I don't know was walking the path that cuts through the back of the yard and leads to a pond deeper in I had noticed the boy's striking posture and looks with a kind of Aschenbachian absorption when I had seen him on a tennis court or when he jogged the roads On this day I had at first not seen the girl with him Maybe she had hidden herself or had come from another direction and I suspected them of a secret meeting because they embraced and leaned away from each other with love-smiles and their arms still around each other's necks How long has it been now since I have been able to smile that way?

The mind does not remember that what satisfies also torments.

I absently move across the room, thinking that I should probably go clean the ashes from the fireplace in the house, but instead I stop in front of one of my paintings on the wall. I tilt my head to see the ratios of space and am satisfied except for the blank white which dominates the color. My *idea* was right; there is strength and movement in what I have done, but the effect of the whole is not there because there is no whole. I often think of Michelangelo's unfinished slaves as being more brilliant than the David because they seem to be struggling to take shape from the rock. Timeless becoming. But something is different here.

I go back to the window.

"Have to put insulation in along the seams," the plasterer says, as if I had questioned what he was doing.

He is perhaps younger than I had first thought, and I wonder what kind of a future he sees in his business. I can imagine him spending his entire life at his work, and yet for myself I cannot see beyond a single day.

He stuffs insulation into the wounds beside the window and then begins to fill the cracks with plaster.

"You lived here long?" he asks.

"No."

"Not too thrilled, huh? Me, I'd have loved to have this house. I could have done a million things here. Parties, you know? This would be really something for parties."

"My husband doesn't like parties."

"Well, you know, I can take 'em or leave 'em. I like a good party once in a while. I mean here you can have a good one, looks to me."

I try to remember the circumstances when we moved in, but the nightmare does not surface readily. I work toward it, as if struggling toward the surface of a lake, thinking

Richard wanted to get out of the city He argued that it was for my own good to get some quiet I was exhausted and the notion of peace just the idea of it gave me some hope And he said that I could use the isolation of the country better than I had used turmoil He found the house bought the furniture had all the dreams   His affection was genuine helping me adjust and seeing him so sure made it difficult to resist I am swayed by time Once I reach a point I see that there is no turning back no chance to change my mind inevitable I am led along as if by desire.

I resist now in my mind. I hate the studio, the low ceilings, the coziness. This was to have been my salvation, but it seems more like compensation, a child's reward for doing what he has been told. Moving was a terrifying step backward, as though now I had to relive the most vivid tortures to gain a new sense of self. I suppose now I have come to accept the place out of sheer will. Such a seemingly small shift in the balance of forces has yielded a radical change in character. Richard's resolve to help me leaves me free to indulge my madness.

"These paintings yours?"

The plasterer is likable if only for his attempts to get me to talk. I do not mind as long as I can safely avoid saying much.

"Yes."

He pauses in his work and looks over the canvasses that are hanging around the room. "I wanted to be a painter," he says, "but I never had the money."

Why shouldn't I believe him? Anyone might have the talent to be a painter. But there is a difference between wanting to be a painter and wanting to paint. I let him go on believing.

He looks from the paintings to me and I wonder if he sees a correlation between the two. The artist and the work. He smiles.

His face now is speckled with white. His white overalls do not show anything. But even his eyes seem speckled like eggs.

I turn away feeling the pressure of his smile. Out the window there is still nothing. The pattern of trees, leaves sodden and heavy on the ground, weeds and grass yellowed and gone to seed. In this apparent chaos one is supposed to find order, immutable laws: water running to the sea, pollen floating in the air, utilization of sunlight in endless cycles.

Before I met Richard I lived with six cats in New York City. I slept on a mattress on the floor of a two-room apartment. The room where I slept was windowless and had a sink in a corner and a stove which gave me heat. It was in the other room, where I had my work, that I began to speak as though everyone in the world were in the same room with me.

My psychiatrist said I was not really sick, but rather that I dwelled upon morbid dreams. What was the difference? He said it was not good for me to be alone all the time.

"I lose friends," I told him. "I say what I think."

"Why do you say what you think?"

"I paint what I think."

"You are not painting in a friendship. Use diplomacy. Smooth over rough situations."

"What about truth?"

He smiled as though I had made a joke. "Concentrate less upon truth. It is impossible to know the truth of anything."

"The truth shall make you free," I argued.

"The truth shall make you crazy."

I shook my head, disbelieving.

"We are committed to a world of appearances," he said.

"It's dishonest."

"It's practical. Think about it." He folded his hands. "Millions have religion as truth, but no religion is true in an absolute sense. Faith answers questions that people feel must be asked and which cannot be answered satisfactorily by their knowledge of the world. You're free from asking questions. You're free of having no answers and can go on doing your job."

"And that's healthier?"

"Yes."

I said, "Yea, though I walk in the valley of the shadow of death, I fear no evil for Thou art with me. And even if Thou art not with me, it is healthier to believe Thou art there somewhere."

"Yes," he said again.

And I said, "I can't do it."

That was about the time I met Richard.

In the beginning he solved my life because he was a truth to believe in, or at least a moral force. He did not mind my explanations, and although he was shocked at how I lived, he seemed to grasp that I was trying to maintain some kind of precipitous balance in my life.

Our first days together were almost impermissible in their beauty. He took time off from his laboratory and virtually kidnapped me to drive with him down to coastal Virginia. It was warm spring, the season of migration of birds. We walked white beaches, swam naked in the chilly water, watched the whirling teal as their green wings caught the sun. Nothing was sacred, and we felt free, making love together in a diamond light.

It was not until later, after we were married, that I began to think that one of his purposes in life was to make me happy. It seemed at first like a positive thing, what anyone in love would want to do for the other person. But to do that, he had to explain me to his satisfaction, and he started using his scientific methods to test my reactions to situations and events. I suspected that he was experimenting upon me the way he did in his laboratory with small animals. It was his firm opinion that everything in the world was discoverable and every action subject to rational analysis. But happiness had never been the object of my life.

Time measures us and makes us smaller. After the first days I slowly slipped back to my flights of insanity, trying to establish some new foundation for my work. We moved my things into his apartment, and although he was patient with my torments and as loving as ever, it was never again the same for me.

It seems now as though I have known Richard only a few minutes, he is such a stranger to me. Always he is the same, always the scientist. What is true is that I am the stranger to him. His methods have yielded nothing, for I keep things hidden. Ideas come to me and vanish and he never learns of them. I do not tell him what I see at the window, for instance, because I don't want him to know. I have my own world of dreams.

I watch the plasterer as he lifts his spatula to the window, spreads plaster, smooths it so that all that is left are a few bubbles on the wet surface. I can feel the worst of the draft has already been stopped. For a moment he pauses, his spatula in midair, and I am struck by the honesty of his gaze. He climbs two rungs on the ladder. He has a dancer's body: thin hips, long legs, wide shouders.

"Do you exercise?" I ask without self-consciousness.

"Handball," he says. "I play handball. Gutsy game."

I imagine him sweating in a small room, shirtless, making noises with his effort and breath. My father used to play a similar game in the streets when he was taking care of me. Richard jogs.

"How long have you been married?"

"To Richard?"

"Is that his name?"

"About three years. Why?"

"You don't seem very happy."

His observation is sincere, which frightens me. I am tired of honest people; I have tried too hard.

"Are you?" I ask.

He smiles again. "I make good money."

I do not know his name, which is a blessing. When I know the name of a tree or a flower in the backyard I somehow cease to notice it. And here is this dancer with speckled blue eyes. I feel my face flush with excitement.

I think of painting this form taking shape before me. The motives for his questions do not concern me, that is, the fact that he looks at me without conscience.

"You don't think money is very important," he says.

"Why do you say that?"

"Your reaction."

I had not been aware that I had reacted. "Money is a necessary evil," I say softly.

"What do you think . . .?"

"Dreams." The quickness of the word surprises me, uttered involuntarily.

"What?"

I do not answer except to say, "I was only talking to myself."

I wonder why I have stayed in this room which I avoid when I'm alone. Is it simply that I am not alone, or am I drawn to a memory? The past seeps through the hard shell of my consciousness as air has once come through the walls of his room and I go back to

the day when my father took me to see a friend of his Gerry Lennox out in Brooklyn when I was seventeen Gerry was a quiet man it seemed to me the kind you'd like to have as a friend if you needed a friend He was a man of good humor taller than my father but not really tall I remember his arms the veins and the way the muscles would define themselves when he lifted a chair Not truck drivers' arms but the arms of a sculpture My father had some business and I agreed to stay with Gerry Lennox who promised to take me for a walk in the park because the day was so warm We set a time to meet in a restaurant But as soon as my father left as I watched him below me cross the street Gerry came up behind me and put one of his forearms under my chin and snapped my head back Don't scream I heard his whistling breath against my skin You're lovely lovely lovely I struggled but there is no worse terror than to be helpless His hand found its way inside my blouse not hard or too eager but soothing He pressed his knees suddenly against the backs of my legs and I went down Lovely lovely He used only the force he needed Not want to scare you Lovely.

The plasterer comes down the ladder, which creaks under his weight. I think of Richard. He is so used to estimating my moods, which are, for me, all deceptions. How would a scientist take betrayal? Would he analyze or would he react?

"Are you all right?"

The plasterer descends, stands close to me. He seems now more real: skin smooth wrinkled splotched. He takes off his cap and scratches his head with the back of his hand.

I don't answer.

"I'm done," he says.

I look at the wall, the window, joined now. I sense movement beyond the glass, look, see the brown and white shape of a deer running, the whole shape never visible because of the trees.

"Look."

He takes two steps, but the deer has gone.

For a moment we stand close to each other in silence. I feel the room tighten, suffocating me. I know what he is thinking, know it would take only one small gesture from me to say yes. Just one touch.

But I turn away.

"Do you want coffee?" I ask.

He hesitates but says, "No, thanks. I've got a couple more jobs this morning."

I close my eyes.

In a moment I hear him packing up his materials, moving the ladder off the cloth on the floor. Even though I am not looking I can see what he does. He gets water from the sink, cleans his spatula. Then he gathers together a few things to carry out to his truck.

He does not close the door. The breeze blows the door back against a chair, and the room chills quickly.

He comes back, closes the door.

"Do you want me to send a bill, or do you want to pay now?" he asks.

His voice seems disembodied, as though I have lost my eyesight and am confronting a gray room.

He stares at me, and I ask, "What do you see?"

He looks sheepish, nervous. "I see you, Mrs. Leiden."

I want to ask him what that means, what he really sees, what details, but instead I say, "Send me a bill if that's all right."

"Sure." He writes something down.

Then he comes across to the window again to collect the ladder.

I try to breathe calmly.

He folds the ladder, but something catches and it does not mesh; he opens it and tries again, this time fitting the sides together perfectly. He picks it up, pauses, looks at me, grins pressing his lips together,

Lovely I feel the weight of Gerry Lennox over me pinning me just in case while he removes my clothes He unfastens every button careful not to tear It is not enough to push my skirt up He must have me nude himself nude I've never seen anyone like you Lovely My mind fills with colors all reds and blues and yellows like a vase full of flowers I can feel the soft touch of his skin he is softer than I His arms and hands like polished stone He does not need to hold me The colors swirl mixed together with a terrible intensity explode He does not need to hold me He lifts up so that I can breathe puts himself close Tries Lovely lovely He looks at me up and down puts a hand on my breast I feel him catch feel him start in feel him swallowed up feel a surge inside He does not need to hold me He stays presses himself against me kisses my cheek puts his fingers against my lips He turns over and pulls me with him and now slowly expands as I raise up The thrill I bite my lip sense my own body's breaking loose from the mooring of the soul.

The plasterer walks across the room and I follow.

I do not understand why I have never painted my dreams. Sometimes I wake in the middle of the night beside Richard and see a river running. It flows into a deep gorge, rushing over rocks, the sunlight breaking from its surface. And there are the same colors that once turned me crazy. It is a river of paint and in this dream of hues I run beside it, screaming and screaming. I want to stop that river, but I don't know why. I want to stop the river that runs colors and *hold it,* but the colors are beyond my grasp, and I watch them descend into the gorge, as if unmoving, caught in the light of the sun.

I stand for a moment on the doorstep beside the plasterer. He is still holding the folded ladder. He smiles. Then he walks out to the truck.

I watch the truck go down the drive and disappear along the curving road. Then I go back to the window where I wait for something to happen in the shadows of the woods, where I spend my time waiting for Richard to get home.

To Go Unknowing

I. A New Mexican Town

The beginning of the dry summer was already in the air. Marcos could feel the heat of the sun. Perspiration rolled down the dark skin of his face and under the arms of his shirt. He walked slowly, looking down at the ground.

He walked a mile and a half from his mother's adobe house to the town. The dust had sifted like flour over his dark tennis shoes. Dust was everywhere in the valley. Though Marcos usually thought nothing of the dust, today he noticed it and became tired of seeing it.

"Marcos, hey!"

The sound of his name rang close to him. He looked up and saw his friend, Jaime, on the sidewalk.

"You've walked right by me," he said to Marcos.

Marcos had been with Jaime through high school, and for the last two years they had worked many of the ranches of the valley together as fruit pickers. Jaime was shorter and had a broad easy smile.

"I had to walk in," Marcos said, as though to explain the dust which covered him. Marcos wiped his broad forehead and tried to smile. "The truck needs a new distributor cap."

He did not have to say how important the truck was to him. It was hard enough for him to get away from his brother, but without the truck it was impossible.

"It's a long way in," Jaime said. "You could have called me. I would have driven out for you."

Jaime's voice was chastizing. Marcos had felt it that way before in the last week whenever he had made some slip. They had always thought of themselves as brothers, ready to do anything for the other. But Marcos could not help it that his mind wandered, nor could he help the change in himself.

Jaime sighed. "I know there is much to consider," he said. "I envy you. But let's not let it come between us."

"It won't." But of that, too, Marcos was uncertain. "All I want now is something cold to drink."

There was one drive-in on the far side of town, and to reach it Marcos had to walk an extra quarter-mile. Costo's Cafe, on the closer side, sold cold drinks, too, but Marcos had not stopped there.

"Not Costo's?" Jaime asked.

"I didn't want to see him," Marcos said. "And I don't want to make conversation with any of the old people."

It had been a hard decision, and Marcos did not want to discuss anything about it. The old people would talk of the past and tell him that he was too young. They would all praise him for helping his mother while she was sick, and they would replay his glory days in high school. Marcos did not want to hear any of it.

"Can you wait a few minutes?" Jaime asked. "I have an errand, and then I'll go with you."

Marcos waited on the street. He felt the burden of being alone more keenly now. He tried to remember, as he stood there, to keep his head up so that he would notice all the people he knew in the town. He knew they would be watching him and waiting for him to say something; they would watch for some sign from him.

His head dropped involuntarily toward the ground again, as his thoughts kept drifting away to the time approaching. He knew they were all judging him, but he could not help it. He must get used to that, he thought. He had never before had to learn to be alone.

That Saturday morning the town seemed very quiet to Marcos. It was as though everything had suddenly become still, like the hesitation before one of the infrequent storms over the valley. He raised his head once, in anticipation of the clouds, but the sky was clear and blue and stretched endlessly along the valley. Only to the west, where the Sangre de Cristo Mountains rose up, did the sky seem to stop. Marcos did not look at the mountains: he did not want to be reminded.

For Marcos had been chosen. There had been weeks of circumspect mutterings, of discussions in backyards and in small adobe rooms far into the night. No one knew exactly who the elders were who chose, or how they decided. They were townspeople and neighbors, but no one seemed to know. Everyone only knew who had been chosen.

It was a great honor to be chosen. It meant that among all the young men for many miles around, from many towns, he had been judged the most able. Yet Marcos dreaded the day of the future, and he had ever since he had earned the grace.

"What do you want?" Jaime asked Marcos.

"Orange with shaved ice."

Marcos slouched back against the seat of Jaime's old Dodge, while Jaime gave the orders through the crackling speaker. He waited for Jaime to pull his head back inside.

"Have you heard anyone talking?" Marcos asked.

"Just the old things," Jaime said cheerfully.

"What do they say? Tell me the truth." Marcos looked seriously at his friend.

"I don't hear much. They all have their doubts. Every five years they have their doubts. But what does it matter?"

"They think I'm not worthy."

Jaime smiled his broad smile. "You're not going to fall."

"Quarres' brother fell. He was bigger than I am. And what about Costo?"

Quarres had been one of their classmates, and his brother had died. But Costo was the worse one for living. Every time you looked at Costo you remembered that he had been chosen too.

"It doesn't happen every time," Jaime said. "It depends on your psyche."

"But they're all thinking it will happen."

"To them it is joyous," Jaime said.

Marcos made a wry face. He thought back to the day he had learned that he was among those being considered. He had been called to the church one day, away from his job on one of the ranches. It had been a cloudy day and cool for the valley; they had hoped for rain, but it had not come. Father Miguel had sent a messenger by truck, and the father had met them at the steps of the mission church.

"We cannot talk well here," Father Miguel said, when Marcos had kneeled and kissed his hand.

They had walked out away from the adobe mission toward the mountains. Marcos was glad they had stayed outside. Yucca and cactus and sage grew over the dry land where they walked.

"You know that Easter is coming," Father Miguel had begun.

"Two weeks from this Sunday," Marcos had answered.

"This is again the fifth year."

"Everyone is talking of it," Marcos said. "At the ranch they have been joking about it for weeks now."

Father Miguel had stopped and had looked at him. "For you it is not a joke. You are among those who may be chosen."

The force of these sudden words had taken Marcos by surprise. Though the thought of it had occurred to him briefly, as it occurred to any young man in the valley, Marcos had never envisioned himself as being the one chosen.

Marcos regained his composure slowly. "They will not choose me," he said.

"Everyone believes they will not choose him," Father Miguel said sternly. "But what if you are the one chosen?"

Marcos considered it. But he knew the elders would not choose him. It was true that he had distinguished himself during his school years. He had received high marks and had nearly gone out of the valley to college in Albuquerque. But he had stayed on to help his mother who had been sick for three long years. Marcos gave her his earnings.

For this they had called him brave and even noble. Marcos had never minded. He did not mind working. His mother showed her gratitude. Perhaps she held him too much, but usually she allowed him to take the truck if he told her he was going with Jaime.

Marcos knew all this spoke well of him. But there was another side of which he had not told anyone yet, not even Jaime. Perhaps everyone knew; perhaps one of the elders knew, for the secrets of the valley were erratically kept. He had never confessed it to Father Miguel, and Marcos had not been about to tell him then.

"You must not accept," Father Miguel said strongly, when Marcos had not answered. "You must tell them you listen to the Church alone."

Marcos had known of the position of the Church, as all boys knew of bitter rivalries. "I don't know," he said hesitantly. "It would be a terrible decision."

"You must not." Father Miguel's voice turned to pleading. "For the Church's sake, Marcos, be the first to renounce them. Look at what they've done. Look at Manny Costo. It has gone on for too many years."

Marcos had listened to the slow, confident voice of Father Miguel. Father Miguel had been one of the staunchest critics of the rites ever since he had come to the valley thirty years before. Marcos had listened to his practiced and eloquent denunciation, just as he had listened every Sunday in the church with his mother to Father Miguel's futile prayers.

"Everyone talks of it," Marcos said, when Father Miguel turned to him at last.

"But they don't know anything. They don't understand. We have come farther than that in this century."

"I suppose not knowing . . . that's what draws us all," Marcos said.

Marcos thought of the unknowing. No, he did not understand precisely what the rites meant. No one had really described them to him, and very few had ever been into the mountains on that Saturday before Easter. The elders allowed no interference. Manny Costo had never spoken of it. That was what fascinated Marcos: no one would be there, and he could break away, without understanding, without the burden of the future.

"He'll fall like a fly," Reynaldo Quarres said. "That will be proof enough."

"And your brother was a sinner of great renown," Jaime countered. "Is that what you mean?"

Reynaldo Quarres was tall and strong like his brother and had himself wished for the chance to avenge his brother's death. "My brother died at the very end," Reynaldo said.

"You were there, I suppose?" Jaime taunted.

"I've heard it told. Marcos will never reach the end."

Marcos was sitting on the table top, one tennis shoe on the bench. Jaime turned away from Reynaldo Quarres, and walked over. Reynaldo shouted something after him.

"You'll see," Jaime said across the parking lot.

Marcos finished the orange slush. He shifted his feet on the bench, leaving odd prints of dust. "I've been thinking of backing out," Marcos said.

"You're crazy," Jaime said, smiling. "Don't let Reynaldo bother you."

They got up together and went toward the truck.

"At least I should tell them everything, and give them a chance to find someone else."

"What haven't you told them? What haven't you told me?"

"Of Dolores," Marcos said.

"What about her?"

Dolores was the rich slummer of the valley, the daughter of one of the wealthiest ranchers.

Marcos was quiet.

"Not you, too?" Jaime said in a low voice.

Marcos nodded. "I don't care," he said. "I'll tell them."

"You can't back out," Jaime said. "If you told them, they would make you go through with it for certain. You wouldn't come back."

"Perhaps that's fair," Marcos said.

"Fair?" Jaime was astonished. "What do they care about being fair?" His eyes narrowed. "You don't believe in the rites, do you?"

"No," Marcos answered quickly. "But maybe there is something to paying the price."

"Come on," Jaime said scornfully.

"What do we know about it?" Marcos insisted.

"You haven't done anything wrong," Jaime said.

"All I know," Marcos said, "is that Manny Costo's wife said that he still wakes up in the night screaming."

Marcos had insisted upon walking the mile and a half home again. He had Jaime let him off in the middle of town. The thought of Manny

Costo intrigued him, and he decided to walk by and look into the back door of the cafe. That way he might see Manny without talking to the others in front.

He walked the back street of the small town, where the tumbledown businesses kept their piles of cartons and their junk. Most of the owners lived in the same place as their small stores, either in back or upstairs. When he had been younger, Marcos had wanted to own his own store in the town. He would have chosen a clothes store, and would have stocked the new peg-leg trousers instead of blue jeans, and perhaps something besides the boots everyone wore. He still thought of it, now and then, but it always seemed a little beyond his reach. His mother was against it, and since he gave her most of his money, he couldn't put up the capital.

The heat rose off the road in waves. Far down the road behind him a car was coming. No one travelled the road behind the stores except the owners and the ones who did not want to be seen. But the car was going fast, he could hear the roar of it, and he turned around. The engine stripped down into second gear, slowing the car, and dust swirled high into the air. When the dust had carried away, Dolores rolled down the window of her Impala and leaned out.

"I just saw Jaime, and he said you told him," Dolores said. "I thought you didn't want anyone to know."

Marcos looked at her. He could almost feel her breath, even in the hot air. She was a terrible dark beauty, used to having her way. There were stories of her running away from college with a man, and other stories of parties she had broken up. He always remembered the sly looks she had given him, the way she hesitated before she looked him straight in the eye, and then the way she turned away just before she passed.

Now, leaning out of the window of the car, she gave him that same look, her dark eyes half-turned away from him, smiling at him.

"I had to tell him," Marcos said.

"But no one else?"

"No."

She laughed. "Because they'll punish you more. It is true that you have been chosen? That's what I've heard from the men at the ranch. It's terrible," she said gaily. "What am I to do?"

Marcos could not answer.

"Is that why you haven't seen me in the last week? Marcos, you're so young." She laughed at him again, putting her head on her hand.

He saw that she looked down at his tennis shoes.

"I was repairing the truck today," he said in explanation. He held up the distributor cap he'd bought. He did not know why she made him feel as though he ought to explain.

"And will it run by tonight?" she asked.

Marcos did not want to say that it would, and he did not want to admit that it wouldn't. Finally he said, "No."

"Come out at ten o'clock," she said. "I'll meet you at the bridge where the sand creek is. No one will see your lights from there."

"I can't," Marcos said. "You know it."

"Tell your mother the same thing," she said.

"It's not my mother."

Dolores smiled and turned her eyes. "It's terrible what they've done to you," she said. "They've made you afraid. You come and I'll make you feel better. Don't be afraid of that."

She smiled at him once more, and then leaned back into the car. She did not give him a chance to answer. The Impala engine roared up, and she churned the dust into the air where it hung now, like Marcos, in the heat.

Manny Costo sat in the back of the cafe with a flyswatter in his hand. There was not much business at eleven in the morning, and he just sat there in the kitchen, nodding his head, waiting for the flies to come to him. He had on a dirty apron and a white T-shirt. A tattoo, "Juarez," curved over his large bicep. He looked up suddenly when Marcos' shadow appeared in the open doorway.

Marcos saw in his eyes a wavering, as though something had triggered there in the deep darkness.

"Who is it?" Manny said.

Marcos stepped inside the door into the kitchen. The sun struck Manny's face. Marcos had not seen Manny Costo for a long time. He had purposely stayed away from Costo's after he had talked to Father Miguel, knowing that Manny had been there. And once chosen, Marcos had not wanted to see Manny Costo at all.

Manny had been chosen fifteen years before, and he had never been the same again. Once he had been fit and full of life, and youth had given him health and good fortune. He had inherited the cafe and had wanted to remodel it and build up the place. But he had never done it, because he had been chosen.

Some said his experience had turned him cruel with the years and that he no longer believed in anything; others said he simply did not care, that he had accepted everything. He seldom spoke to anyone. He cooked in the dirty kitchen while his wife took orders and brought the slips to the little window.

For a long moment Manny was silent, staring at Marcos with his deep black eyes. His look was almost wild, and Marcos wondered whether he ought to have come. Then Manny leaned forward and pulled himself slowly from the stool where he sat. He stood up with effort, lurching to the side. His left leg was shortened where it had been cut off, and he grasped tightly at the railing he had built for himself around the kitchen. He had always refused crutches, and yet without them he could not leave the cafe. With heavy arms, he held his balance, fixing his gaze on Marcos.

Manny took two hesitant steps forward, more pulling himself along the railing than stepping. He kept his balance, edging closer toward Marcos.

For an instant Marcos wished to help him, to hold out his hand and to take the man's arm. But he did not. He stood as quietly as he could, heart beating, and he waited.

Manny edged closer, and at last leaned out away from the railing. He was almost close enough to touch Marcos if he had held the railing and reached out one arm. But instead he balanced there, letting go of the railing, tottering; and then he fell forward and threw his arms around Marcos.

Marcos felt the bristly skin of Manny's face against his own, felt the weight of the man leaning upon him, felt the warmth of him. Marcos, too, put his arms up, around Manny, holding him. They held that way for a long moment, Manny clinging and, at last, crying.

Finally Manny leaned back on his one good leg, the wet skin of his face shining.

In the pain of that look Marcos knew that he could not ask. He knew that it would go hard for him. He knew that it had never been cruelty in Manny's eyes, that Manny's silence had never been to lock the others out. Instead it had been because he knew something he could never express. Marcos did not understand even then whether it was a deep bitterness or a deep love. Perhaps the two had been merged in the years of continuing, the duty, the running of the cafe in the small town, watching the frailty and the pathetic lives which passed by him.

Manny backed away and this time Marcos helped him. Manny stood at his railing while Marcos backed out into the sunlight. They did not speak.

The old truck started. The hood shook violently above the engine as Marcos leaned over it. Then he let the hood fall with a loud crash. He was satisfied with his work.

His mother came out onto the steps. She was a small woman and seemed incapable of bearing a son like Marcos. Her dress was clean and new, and there was a rosary around her neck.

"Don't be late now," she said.

"All right," Marcos answered, climbing into the pickup.

"Early Mass tomorrow morning," she said. "Father Miguel . . ."

"I know," he interrupted. The next day was Palm Sunday, and Father Miguel would expect him.

Marcos put the truck into gear and drove slowly out of the driveway. He turned at the gate and went south toward town.

He did not want to face Father Miguel. He did not want to listen anymore. No one in the town considered truth to be anything except what Father Miguel said. His mother was the worst of them. At the same time that they believed in the truths of the Church, they also believed in the rites. Their hearts differed from their minds. Something more mysterious, more powerful than the God of the Church drew them away. It was as though, all their lives, they had believed in the sun which rose and fell in pattern each day, and then one day, when the moon came between the earth and the sun and cast its shadow upon them, they suddenly and for that short moment believed in the eclipse, in the shadow, in the darkness.

Marcos did not want to have to explain this to Father Miguel. He did not want to have to say why it was that he had accepted.

He kept driving. At the town he turned off and took the back road behind the stores. He did not know what to believe himself. He had wanted to ask Manny Costo what to believe, but he could not ask. It would have been cowardice to have asked.

Marcos checked his watch. Dolores had said 10 o'clock, and it was only 9:15. The sky had already turned dark overhead, but there remained a soft brilliance of blue light over the mountains where the sun had disappeared. The stars eased out.

Dolores' arms. He had not confessed of them. Dolores smiling up at him. If anyone knew . . . or did they know? No, he thought, for they would not have chosen him. He imagined Dolores' soft body lying in the bed of the truck. They had huddled together in the cool night, absorbed. She had not coaxed him, not really. He thought of the terrible penalty, the wages of sin, which Father Miguel had often lectured about. But he had never felt guilt. Instead he had felt stronger, surer.

He turned back onto the main road after the town and followed it south. After a few miles he turned again onto one of the dirt roads to the west. He drove slowly. About half a mile before the bridge over the sand creek, he turned off his lights and edged through the darkness. It was easy to see the tan stripe of dusty road even on the darkest of nights.

He was frightened of his capacity and his weakness. What if he did fall? He had accepted the honor, and yet there was Dolores. He felt he had no strength to turn back, and none to go on. He had kept her hidden from them all, like a child who is afraid of his own evil.

He saw the silver bridge ahead of him in the darkness. He was early. He swung the truck over to the side of the road and stopped. The engine died, and the quiet night descended.

From the glove compartment he took a small bottle of whisky, poured out a capful, and drank it off. It burned. Then he lay back, his head against the seat of the cab.

He could see Dolores as she approached. The bridge over the sand creek was in a draw, and the road to the Montez ranch turned off the dirt road at the top of the hill. Now she came along that road, a black figure against the sky.

She came up to his side of the cab and looked in. Marcos sat up and opened the door. She kissed him hurriedly.

"Hey," he said softly, breaking away, "I shouldn't have come, you know that? I only came because I knew you'd be here."

"You don't have to whisper," she said aloud, laughing. He could see her smiling at him in the dark. "Marcos, you are so young. Here, give me some."

She held out her hand for the bottle.

"I can't stay," he said, raising his voice a little, as he watched her tilt the bottle to her mouth. His voice sounded so loud to him in the darkness.

"It's Saturday night," Dolores said. "Everybody is already in town. We can be alone out here. Drive up a little, over the hill." She turned to him. "You're not afraid, are you?"

She was still outside in the darkness.

"I'm not afraid," Marcos said.

"We can lie on the sand down in the creek bed."

Marcos poured another cap for himself. "Get into the truck," he said.

Dolores went around the hood to the other side. Marcos leaned across the seat and clicked the door open. Dolores climbed up.

He started the motor. It coughed loudly and then settled down. He wheeled the truck around, backed up, and then headed back in the direction of the town.

"Where are we going?" she asked, moving across the seat toward him. "I thought you wanted me."

"I do," he said. "But first we're going to town."

Marcos went down the aisle of the mission church with his mother. She had wakened him at 6:30, and, as they were every Sunday, they were early. His mother said she liked to get there way ahead to have time to think of God and not of the people.

In the aisle she kneeled and made the sign of the cross over herself. Marcos hesitated, and then he, too, kneeled. He had his hand in front of him, but he did not make the sign of the cross.

It was a small adobe mission. The inside walls were whitewashed, and light shone through thick slits in the walls. In the early days of the Spanish settlers, the soldiers had fired upon the Indians from those slits. At the front of the church, above the altar, hung a large wooden cross with a carving of Jesus nailed to it. A man in the valley had sculpted the Jesus years ago from a piece of pine, and now the colors had faded and chipped. The white of the clothing had turned brown as the wood; the skin was brown; the halo flecked with gold.

Marcos let his mother sit on the aisle so she could see the altar. She kneeled before her seat and began praying. Marcos sat and looked at the carving of Jesus.

He had seen it many times before in indifference, but now a strange feeling welled up in him. The sculptor had tried to give Jesus' face a look of deep torment, but he had succeeded only in making a sad-eyed mask. Marcos had expected to feel something new that day. But he felt, not the love or the pity he expected, but rather a sense of indignation. He knew he ought to have felt kinship and identity with the Christ, for he had been chosen. He had been chosen to be the Christ in the rites. But he did not feel as he was supposed to feel. He felt only lost, and he wondered why he had to sit there in the church and suffer this.

The people had started coming in in greater numbers. Some of them looked at him, and Marcos wondered whether those same eyes had seen him in the town with Dolores. There had been many people there, and he and Dolores had drunk a good deal at several places, even at Costo's. Marcos wondered whether those eyes would stare at him through eyeslits on the night of the rites.

He turned nervously in his seat. His mother was still kneeling, eyes closed, her dry mouth moving rapidly. She whispered so loudly that Marcos could nearly hear her words. Her face broke into lines as she mouthed her prayer, and he hated her for praying for him.

He sat upright. Dolores came down the outside row to his right, followed by her parents. Her dark face was posed so seriously. When her eyes caught Marcos', she gave a soft smile. Marcos could see the smile beneath the veil over her eyes.

His head whirled with thoughts. He saw in Dolores such sweetness where everyone else saw putrefaction. She was afraid of nothing.

He looked away from her. On the altar below the Christ carving, a small boy in a long white robe was lighting the many candles.

Marcos stood up suddenly.

The church was crowded now. People kneeled in the center aisle and crossed themselves. Over and over again. It seemed to him that each of them looked at him when he had stood up.

His mother pulled at his hand. "Marcos," she whispered.

He pulled his hand away roughly. Then he stepped behind her into the aisle. He made his way this way and that through the crowd of those who were kneeling and those who were waiting to kneel.

II. The High Country

The elders came for him at midnight the following Friday.

They drove into the yard of Marcos' adobe house in a large truck, and they entered the house without knocking. Over their heads they wore brown hoods, like monks, their eyes peering through slits.

Marcos awoke with his mother's scream. He could hear her pleading in the living room. "Please, do not take him! Please. What will I do?"

Marcos came out of his room, and the elders took hold of his arms. They paid his mother no attention, and merely tightened their grasp upon him when she begged them for him. Finally they pulled him out of the house and into the night.

In the yard they covered his head with a brown cloth. There were no holes for the eyes. Then they helped him into the truck where he sat shivering in the cold. One of the elders put a cloak around him. No one said a word. Every one of them seemed to know what to do.

The truck rumbled heavily out of the yard and onto the highway. There were many men in the back with Marcos. He could feel the weight of their breathing. He did not know how many there were, but it was a large truck, like the ones he had seen carrying soldiers at Los Alamos. They sat on the flatbed of the truck, huddled together, waiting.

Marcos knew that they had driven northward out of the gate. He could feel the glide of truck on the paved highway. As long as they were on pavement, he could imagine the country. He knew the valley well in the light. But after a while, in the darkness, he became confused. He tried to keep track of time and speed, but it was useless.

Then the truck slowed, turned west, and picked up speed again. Gravel slithered under the wheels, and they all breathed the dust which the truck blew up. Now Marcos was lost; there were too many small roads leading west into the mountains.

They seemed to go forever. His heart raced. In the closeness of his own breathing inside the hood, Marcos thought. All the things he should not have done! All the things he had done without thought of consequence! Now he would pay for them. But under the hood he smiled.

The truck slowed again and began to climb. Marcos thought of the mountains, rising high, full of canyons, valleys, and trails. There were so many pockets in the mountains that he knew no one could find them. And the elders made certain that no one ever followed.

The truck heaved, paused while the driver shifted down, and then kept climbing. The men in the flatbed were jostled against each other, but no one cursed. They all seemed to have much patience.

Finally the truck stopped. The men took off Marcos' boots and socks, and helped him off the back. Two of them stood beside him, holding him by the arms. In any case there was no chance to escape. He had taken the oath to accept, to give up his fate to the hands of God, and never to breathe a word of the rites to anyone on penalty of death.

Marcos could hear their muted voices in Spanish. He could not catch their words, or understand what they were doing. Some of the men seemed to be far away in the trees, and others seemed close at hand. Finally he was led along the cold ground; he could feel the pine needles under his feet. But he could not hear the footsteps of the other men. Somewhere behind him he heard a loud voice call, "Until then!", and he heard the truck motor start and the truck pull away. The sound of the motor diminished into the night.

They waited. Marcos could hear more men coming toward them along the trail. A chill went through him as they approached. The truck had disappeared; he did not know where he was; they were about to begin.

All that he had known seemed to come before his eyes and then to vanish. He was in a foreign land, a land travelled by few. He was bound, certain of defeat, yet willing to go on.

The footsteps of the men stopped near him. The two men who had been holding him at last let him go, and one of them removed the hood which had covered his eyes.

Marcos saw candles in the darkness. There were three of them, held by elders. These lighted a circle of men who surrounded him in the clearing of the forest. Beyond this circle, the tall black pines rose up to the moonless sky overhead. Marcos turned. He counted five rifles, but there may have been more. The golden, flickering light of the candles glinted off the barrels. Marcos knew no one would try to follow. He thought of Jaime, who could not help him now, and he thought of his mother's tears and her praying. Dolores' soft face appeared to him, too, but they were all behind him, and he was glad.

Marcos felt the glare of the men's strange eyes, eyes like animals' which did not understand or care to understand. These men were driven by their vision, and they would carry through that vision, and stop at nothing. Marcos realized then what Father Miguel had meant. It was all from the past, brought up from the caves of old Spain, secreted in mystery, and carried forward.

On the ground before him, nailed together with iron spikes, was a giant cross, twenty feet long and seven wide, roughhewn from pine, with bits of ragged bark still clinging to it. Beside the cross lay a green crown of yucca spires woven together, and a pile of willow switches.

The cold seeped through Marcos' feet as he stood. A thought came to him suddenly, and though he tried to push it away, it stuck in his mind. He tried to think of something else, to recognize some one of the elders, but the thought persisted and came to consciousness. He hated the idea that he was paying through the judgment of God, and he refused to believe it.

One of the men stepped from the rear of the circle and took Marcos' shirt collar forcibly in his hand. He jerked Marcos so suddenly that he gasped for breath. The shirt split down the back, and Marcos stood naked from the waist, the chilly night down upon him, barefooted, confronting his torturers.

One of the elders came forward, took the yucca crown, and approached Marcos. Marcos saw the man's eyes beneath the hood; they seemed yellow and gleaming in the dull light. A chant rose up, and from behind him, a reed flute wailed a haunting series of notes, like a wolf's cry. The elder put the crown on Marcos' head and pressed it down. Marcos could feel the sharp spines of the yucca pierce his skin. Blood oozed down his neck. For an instant Marcos sensed pain, and he vowed to struggle against it. It was in the psyche, Jaime had said. The elder pushed the crown down even more tightly, and then stepped back.

Others came forward for the willow switches. Marcos stood as calmly as he could, fighting his thoughts. He cried out, again and again, in the night, but his cries meant nothing. The chanting went on, and the reed flute wailed.

At last the whipping stopped. Marcos had fallen to his knees. His trousers were soaked with the blood which ran down his back. The elders circled him, kneeled, and began praying loudly.

He was not tied with ropes. He felt like running while he could still run, but he did not. He felt like cursing them, but no words came to his lips.

The elders rose from their knees and took hold of the cross. Three of them lifted it over Marcos and laid it upon his shoulder. The procession was to begin.

The light of day seeped slowly through the forest like a spirit. Marcos longed for daylight; all he wanted was to have light shine upon his torture in the hope that God would see his punishers.

The trees took shape first, without color, their dark forms in contrast to the sky. The two men still walked beside him, and there was a column in front of and behind him along the trail. The men beside him were to help him up when he fell.

He had not fallen by the time it had begun to be light.

"Go slowly," one of the elders had whispered to him. Marcos had tried to separate out this friend, to find an ally, but the man had drawn back into the group.

The blood still oozed from the cuts over Marcos' forehead, but the sweat of his work did not allow it to dry. Sometimes one of the elders would break ranks to lash him with a switch, and periodically one would push the yucca crown deeper into Marcos' matted hair. For a moment the new pain would try him.

But he did not mind the yucca spines, nor the lashes of the willow switches. Those he could bear. They were stings of momentary duration, and he was numbed to them. But not to the steps. Each step was a torment; each step was unbearable suffering with the weight of the cross over him; each step he feared more than death itself.

Though it was bright light, the sun had not yet risen when Marcos bore the cross out of the trees at timberline. They crossed along a ridge and descended into a high valley where the rocks rose up sharply. Snow lay in the crevasses like tongues. Clouds covered the tops of the mountains.

Descending into the valley they crossed a snowfield. Marcos welcomed the coolness on his raw feet. Twice the snow gave way beneath him and he fell forward. The first time he got to his feet alone, but the second time he had no strength. He lurched forward and did not even put his hands out to brace himself for the fall. The cross on his shoulder hung for a second in the air and then fell too, striking him heavily on the back. He lay there.

"You must continue," a voice said beside his ear.

The strange hooded shape loomed up before his eyes. Marcos turned over onto his back; the cold felt good against the heat of his wounds. He wanted to rest there, to disappear beneath the ice of the mountain.

"Why?" he asked.

"Because you are the absolution for us all," the voice said, as though the idea were so clear and fundamental that he had no need to utter it.

Marcos stirred slowly. He did not believe, but he struggled to get up.

"For the love of us all," the voice said.

Marcos did not love. He had been raised, as they all had, in the belief of glory. But he knew at last there was no glory.

"Why?" he asked again, this time to himself. This time, with Manny Costo.

He rose to his knees and then regained his feet. The snow was pink with his blood. He looked around at the elders, who were waiting patiently, their eyes now in the light of day.

"It's not far now," the voice said.

The flute went on.

Marcos did not think of returning. He saw behind him, at the lip of the valley, three of the elders with rifles. They had been left behind to watch for intruders.

The switches began again. He had become so tired that he no longer cared. It was not only the work. He had worked long hours in the fields. But he had never done so much alone. In the fields he had always had Jaime, and then afterwards drinking and the girls. There had always been something to look forward to.

Now he no longer dreaded even the steps.

The ground leveled in the high valley. A small shallow lake, gray from the reflection of the clouds, lay before him. The elders in the column ahead of him swung now in a circle and stopped at a group of rocks. They turned to face Marcos.

He wondered at the sight he must have made. He was bent forward under the weight of the cross. They could see his blood over his face and back. They could see the giant cross they had made for him, and the set of his dry mouth with parched white at the corners.

But they could not see the feelings inside him, nor the ache of his body, nor the throbbing in his head. They could not see the hatred which he felt for them in his heart. He did not care. He was a man; he had carried their cross; he had borne their agony for them.

The sun had risen, but the clouds had not moved. He could not resist them, as they tied him to the cross. Marcos had not believed, even to the very end of his journey, that they would do this final thing. He had heard their rumors; Reynaldo Quarres always had said this was where his brother died. And Marcos had always believed that Manny Costo had lost his leg in the climb. He had never believed this.

When he was bound, they raised the cross, and rolled heavy rocks to its base to support it. Marcos looked down over them with half-closed eyes. He did not know whether he was conscious or not. He slept, and he dreamed.

He dreamed that he was soaring above the trees, half-man, with wings of thirty feet and feathers of silk. He skimmed the tops of the trees and let himself ride through the air on those giant wings, a condor, looking for carrion.

He angled away across an outcropping of rock. The great valley where he lived gradually came to view over a hill. He could see the silver ribbon of a stream below, the light green of high meadow grass, the dark black-green of the trees. He saw no movement in the forest.

Marcos climbed on those wings. He climbed above the snow and above the rocks of the great mountains. The land seemed to flatten out from the height he attained; the land had no depth, but only a great width. It stretched around him, a slight curve at the horizon.

The sun warmed him, warmed the silken wings which carried him.

He had no hurry. The wind currents bore him up easily. He rode them, knowing that the wind could never cease.

He soared down the mountainside, in search, and out over the plain of the valley. He could see the network of roads and wires and the faraway buildings of the town. The plain was light brown, dry. For a long time he saw no life.

Then, as he began to climb again, he saw the child. A mother was working in the fields, a healthy, robust woman beside a remote house. The child played by the house. Marcos' shadow floated black on the ground, but the woman did not look up. Then he swooped with an easy reach, and carried off the child.

The child did not cry. Marcos looked at the smiling face as he held the child and rose. He climbed with strong wings, riding the currents until he was far above the valley plain.

Missing.

Lost.

Marcos carried the child to the mountains. "I am saving you," he said.

The land spread out again from his great height. He drifted over the black of the forest and the gray and white of the high mountains.

Then, over the wild mountains, he let the child slip from his grasp.

Marcos awoke to the screams of the elders. They were stripped and were stinging each other with willows. Chanting; moaning; praying. The flute kept up its haunting voice. Marcos watched through bloody eyes. When they had taken their lashes, they bathed in the snow-fed waters. He could see their dark backs stained with the red welts. The hoods still covered their faces.

He did not know how time passed. It had seemed centuries. The clouds still hung low over the mountains. They seemed to swirl over the rocks and then to float down the valley. He looked up into the vast white-gray world, the mist. He said once, "What am I?"

The elders gathered around him, hearing those words, turning their eyes to him, and kneeling in prayer.

Marcos pitied them, and in his pity he found disgust. Nameless, faceless. He would have denounced them all. He knew that they waited for a word from him; their eyes seemed to beg. And yet he said nothing.

He was too weak. He could scarcely move his head from side to side. He no longer wished to come down from the cross. He had neither aspiration nor desire. Neither love nor hope. Everything had been drawn from him. His head fell to the side, and he lost consciousness.

He awoke once.

Rain swept down the high valley. The rain poured over him, but he did not move. He felt a great joy.

The elders knelt in the rain, looking up to him.

Marcos said nothing.

The rain subsided, and the storm drifted on fast-moving air out across the plain. He thought of the rain in the valley, his home, the water striking the dust of the field and the roads.

Clear air followed the storm. Blue edged over the ridge of the mountains, and then came the sun. It streamed down onto his face, warm against his skin. He felt only that warmth now; he felt no pain. He thought of Manny Costo clinging to the railing in the kitchen. Manny knew, and now Marcos also knew. Never again could he be the same.

It was sunset when the elders took him down.

They laid Marcos on a blanket. He was delirious. He watched them through stark, uncomprehending eyes.

The elders poured kerosene onto the cross and lit a small pile of brush beneath it. The flames soared into the evening sky.

Marcos did not remember the journey down. He recalled only the wailing of the flute in the darkness, and he had been afraid. Vaguely he remembered the truck motor and the rumbling along the road. He did not understand these things. He did not hate them any longer. He loved and hated nothing.

It was nearly midnight again when they delivered Marcos to his weeping mother.

Every Day a Promise

He could not describe the feeling. If he had told anyone, analogy was all he could use: like a blind spot in vision, like trying to catch a fish which was not there, like losing something through a hole in your pocket. He had never thought about it when he was younger because the feeling had never existed then. But it existed now.

Growing up in Hamden, he used to run the narrow, tree-shrouded country roads after school, not because he was in training, but because he wanted to. Even then he'd had his sights set on records. His chest was thin and his body was all knees and elbows, but his legs had always had a piano-wire resilience, that spring.

And he had succeeded: schoolboy records for Connecticut, Ivy records at Yale. He had always felt his talent would be enough to bring him through. When had it begun, that suspicion? He could not point to any moment or hour or day.

The bus on which McCallum was riding stopped, and he climbed down to the pavement. He knew she would be waiting for him, knew that as soon as she saw the bus crest the hill she would start down the lane to meet him. Why should he think that bad?

He paused for a moment, looking after the bus, watching it climb the hill with its exhaust tail swirling in the cold air. Only two years before he had stood in front of that black and white bar at the Nationals. He'd had confidence then. He could be outside of himself and see his own movements, as if on a film clip, moving deliberately back and forth, measuring his own height against that of the bar set several inches above his head. From a standing position he kicked his leg up, testing, and then he walked back in his easy, loping gait. Number 14, New York Track Club, faced the camera without seeing anyone else.

He concentrated like a magician doing a sleight of hand. He had counted his steps to the take-off, knew precisely his stride, momentum, stutter step. He knew everything in the world to know. He knew the movement of his body through the air, the kick of the trailing leg, the exact moment he had to be highest to be over. He turned back and looked for a split second at the bar which was spun like a thread between two posts. And then in the bright sun he had raced forward, springing off his left foot, and he had jumped a height he had only rarely dreamed about.

Hillary waved to him and he felt forced to wave back. He told himself: if you feel that way about her, then tell her. It was true that nothing held him; they weren't married. But what kept coming to his mind was that he could not blame her for the other.

The lane was really an alley shaded by trees. On either side were the garages of the houses, vine-covered so that from the mouth of the lane you could see only green down the slope. McCallum walked slowly, as if tired. She was young, he thought. All that she had been through and still she looked young. Gentle eyes that should have been hard. Deceiving? She could be fierce, too. But the past had not seemed to affect her very much. No fuss, no emotion.

Suddenly from the tangle of underbrush the children sprang out, shouting and laughing. "Uncle Mac, Uncle Mac!"

Surrounded, he threw his hands up in surrender. John, seven, and Marnie, five. In their dark-tanned faces he saw the traces of Hillary as a child, blended with another man he had never seen.

Each of them took one of McCallum's arms, and they led him down the lane to their mother. "We caught him," Marnie shouted.

Hillary embraced him and brushed back her dark hair. She was dressed for the chill in a jacket which hid her figure. The cold had turned her face red.

"We want Uncle Mac to come with us to the park," John shouted.

"See what we found," Marnie put in.

"What is it?"

"You have to *see*," Marnie said, tugging.

"Something dead," John said proudly, as if dead things were more exciting than things alive.

"Uncle Mac has to rest," Hillary said. "He's worked."

"You don't want to come, Uncle Mac?"

He looked at them. "Not now, hey? Maybe tomorrow. If it's dead it won't move."

The children let go of his arms. "Somebody might steal it," John said.

"You children go over to the Harrises for a while," Hillary suggested, reading McCallum's face.

"I don't want to play with *her,*" John said, meaning the Harris child.

"Then find something to do."

Betrayed, the children moved off slowly at first, and then when an idea hit them they broke into a run.

"Do you know I've decided something?" They sat on the comfortable sofa in the living room of her house, but he did not look at her as he spoke. "That is, I've decided something and nothing."

He could feel that she was watching him, sensed her effort not to be too eager to guess anything.

"Well, which is it?"

It was quiet in the house. The children had been asleep for an hour, and he listened for the clock. For a while he did not answer her, his mind running on the trouble with this house.

"Where did you get all these things?" he asked.

"What have you decided?" she asked back.

"Like this glass bird," he said. He stood up and went to the mantle and picked up the heavy figurine. Probably from her ex-husband, he thought. It was a plumed bird, one that never had existed. "Given to you?"

"No, I bought it."

"Where?"

"Buenos Aires."

Buenos Aires. He had been there. Pan American Games. He remembered the crowded stadium, but could not recall how he had done. Her husband had been on some government mission.

"How much?"

Hillary, he could tell, did not like his questions. "I forget," she said impatiently. "From a street peddler. John wanted it."

"Not valuable?"

"I like it for the luck," she said.

He put the bird back on the mantle and turned around. "I've decided it's tomorrow or never."

"What's tomorrow or never?"

"Something or nothing. Tomorrow is the end of the season."

She did not answer, did not move except to give a half-smile which was ambiguous. He knew it was a demand from her to spell out what he meant. Or was that the meaning he attached to her expression? He felt himself stir, as if drifting away from her, a boat from a mooring. Did he mean what he said?

"I can't keep going without believing I'm getting better. It's not enough to hang on and make expenses. I can't . . ." He looked at the subtle ease with which she listened. He should not have come, he thought. He should have stayed in his room and relaxed the night before a meet. He knew she would be silent. She *had* to be silent, yet why didn't she ask him what it was he couldn't do?

"I've set a height for the jumping tomorrow."

This, an admission, he thought, as much a promise as anything he could put into writing.

"Is it what you want to do?"

"It's what I am doing."

"You're not doing this for me," she said. "I don't want you to." She looked at him, smiling lightly. "You always think you know how I feel, but what you think isn't true. I only want you to do what you believe in."

"Not for you," he said, feeling anger rise.

Sometimes that was what he wanted most: he wanted her to say to him that he should quit because he was a fool for jumping when he was too old. There were younger jumpers now who would pass him, new styles, younger jumpers with catapults in their legs, with coaches and money to spend. He should grow up and stop believing that he could do what he had never done and now had no hope of doing. But she would never say that. She always put it back onto him.

Or was that really it? He knew all that. No one knew it better. Wasn't it something else?

He had taken the cellar apartment more than three years ago, when he stopped working for J. R. Guadagno, the investment firm. Seven years past college, he had wanted a last try at the Olympics, and he had planned it to the dollar. He sold his car. Then at the Trials he'd been hurt. Hamstring pull, couldn't jump. The trainers told him all he could do was rest.

It had made sense to go back to Guadagno, but something else began to bother him. He didn't have enough time. He worked only two weeks before he quit for good.

Then he had met Hillary. Running one day along the street, John had ridden his bike up the lane and had nearly hit him at the blind corner. McCallum had caught the bike as the child was about to fall sideways.

"Are you a jogger?" John had asked.

"I'm a jumper."

"But you're running," John insisted.

"I'm training." McCallum had seen the woman coming up along the edge of the green alley.

"You're just talking now," John said.

McCallum smiled.

Thinking back on it, he remembered that she'd mentioned her divorce right away. She had never hidden anything from him. What could she have hidden? It was a court case, a public record. She'd won custody and support, no alimony. She hadn't asked for any because she had money of her own.

Almost immediately after their meeting she'd asked him to move in.

And what had he kept hidden from her? He had not given up his cellar room. It was cheap rent, a place to go when he needed to. It was almost a whim that he continued the secret at first, but then it became a necessity.

"Can the children call you 'uncle'?" she asked.

He acquiesced. They had to call him something. A Yale name, McCallum Pillsbury, reduced to Uncle Mac. A hamburger. He liked the children, played with them, helped them with lessons. But if it had started anywhere ascertainable, it had started with them.

"Uncle Mac, can we watch you jump someday?" John asked.

"Sure."

"When?" Marnie jumped up and down.

"I'll take you to practice."

"I mean a big meet," John said.

"Okay."

"Promise?"

"I promise."

But he had never taken them. Promise. What else had he promised them? Every day was a promise, taking them for ice cream, asking them questions about their school and their friends and their feelings. And every day was a lie.

Hillary encouraged them. "Tell Uncle Mac what you told me," she would say.

And Marnie would spill out a confusion of words and emotions about what had happened to her in the tree house at the neighbor's place, or what she had seen and had never told anyone else.

John would come to him and say, "Mom told me to ask you to show me how to shoot this basketball like a pro."

"Sure."

And he would listen to Marnie's stories and laugh, and he would take the ball and cradle it and kneel down beside John and take John's small hands and put them on the ball inside his.

The nights with Hillary seemed so easy. They would lie in that love-making silence in her bed, the moonlight sifting through the deep trees to her window. He would caress her and she would hold tighter, and he knew that all he had to do for the rest of his life was to say yes. And when he was inside her, he could hear her sighing from some great distance away, feel himself sinking deeper, as though he were disappearing and she were calling to him to stay.

Several hours before the meet, he stopped by his cellar room to pick up a clean sweat suit. He stood for a moment, wondering.

He did not work, yet no one could have been more disciplined. He ran every morning and evening. In the afternoons he went to the athletic club to lift weights: leg presses, bicycle, stretches, isometrics. Then he would jump—just low heights—with lead sewn into the ankles of a specially made pair of shoes.

But now there was the notion that what he did was absurd. All the measuring and fiddling with steps, with take-off angles, with kicks. He had believed implicitly for so long that he could jump higher and higher until he had jumped higher than anyone else had ever jumped. It was an injustice that he had always been off that fraction. Did it matter?

Finally he laid down on the bed, stretching his long frame diagonally across the covers. He breathed deeply, trying to concentrate on the meet. But his mind wandered. A low light came in through the cellar box windows, throwing a dull sheen over the damp room. He tried to think what it might have been that John and Marnie had wanted to show him. A dead what? He imagined a run-over cat dragged to the gutter near the sidewalk. Or a pigeon killed by disease, its iridescent feathers tufted in the wind.

He lay on the bed for an hour until the chill of the unheated room began to cramp his muscles. He was often astonished that he could feel so lonely when he had such a place as Hillary's house to go to, that he could feel hatred when love was everywhere in the three people he went to see. How did he find the green ugly and the house a grotesque configuration of angles and slabs?

He got up to catch the bus.

The infield was filled with movement as he came down the long tunnel from the dressing room. The sun seemed to suspend the colors of the athletes' suits against the green backdrop of the infield, and McCallum felt a new nervousness come over him. After eight years of top competition he should not have been nervous, but it was there. It was not the nervousness of youthful energy or even the ultimatum that he had announced to Hillary the night before. Rather, some other deep wound oozed blood, some awareness that what he was doing was not right.

He stopped at the mouth of the tunnel and looked across the crowd that filled the arena. Hillary had wanted to bring the children, but he had said no.

"Why can't we come, Uncle Mac?" Marnie asked.

"We want to see you." John shook loose from his mother's grip and came over to McCallum standing on the patio porch. "You said once we could."

"When?" John's dark face resembled Hillary's in obstinance.

"I don't know when."

Tears came to Marnie's eyes and she ran from the room.

"I'm sorry," Hillary said. "I shouldn't have told them."

"It's all right."

He jogged down the ramp and out onto the infield. In his blue warm-ups he trotted across to the high-jump area, waving to some of his friends taking calisthentics. The familiar feeling came to him, the warmth of the colors, the milling about in anticipation. He remembered Buenos Aires, the stadium, not the town. Some of the events had already been run, a couple of the sprints, the women's javelin, broad jump. The loudspeaker made a first call for the 880.

At the side of the composition approach he started some slow exercises of his own. The others, mostly younger faces he knew, had already done their calisthentics and were measuring their approaches on the apron. Lying on his back on the grass, McCallum closed his eyes and lifted his legs, spreading them, bringing them together, then lowering them again. He supposed Hillary could have brought the children anyway, hiding them easily in the kaleidoscopic pattern of the crowd. And he supposed she could have discovered that he'd taken her glass-plumed bird from the mantle. If he had asked her she would have said yes, but there would have been questions, maybe jokes. So he had just put it into his satchel.

He did push-ups, ten, fifteen, touching his nose to the grass. The blue warm-ups absorbed the sun, and he felt himself break into a short sweat. Up on his feet, a few jumping jacks, raising his arms and spreading his legs in constant rhythm. He felt as though he were breaking apart, arms legs whirling out into the air.

The younger jumpers had shed their warm-ups, but McCallum waited until the event was called and the competitors introduced. He stayed aloof from the others, concentrated on working out his steps. He was in a grim world then, the fate of everyone who tried to realize dreams. But he felt loose and as strong as ever.

Between practice jumps he sat on the grass. He had taken the figurine out and had put it beside him. A mascot. He had told Hillary he'd set a height for himself, but he had set no height. He no longer knew what to expect of himself. Six feet nine? Seven even? More and more jumpers reached seven. What was good enough after he had spent his whole life believing in himself? When he tried to think of inches, nothing came to him.

He passed on the first two heights, keeping warm by jogging. He stretched anxiously while the other jumpers tried themselves against the bar. At the third height, when his name was called, he stripped off his sweat pants. Once more he walked forward to check his stride to the bar. He gauged his own height. In an exaggerated ritual he walked back again, counting silently.

Then he turned, took a deep breath, and ran. With light stride he hurried up, building momentum. His left foot dug in, he shot up. In a simple movement he kicked and rolled and was over.

He had been good, felt right, and confidence rose in him. He passed again at the next jump and waited. It was all still possible. The sun warmed him and he sat beside the gaudy glass bird and smiled.

He jumped twice more, feeling right, and he knew. The bar was raised again. He was unthinking now, and when he was called, he went up, soared, and cleared.

Hillary would not know which bus he would take, and to make sure she would not meet him, he got off at the stop ahead of the lane. He walked slowly, the neighborhood sifting into darkness before his eyes. Red leaves fell, blown down by sharp gusts of wind. He shouldered his satchel, the weight pressing against his ribs.

It had not been a record that afternoon, but there had been an old feeling. In the instant he had gone over the bar, he had been somehow resurrected, yet it had been a resurrection without joy. He had not ever thought of a bitterness in himself and the tainted feeling it gave his triumph. How could he have known?

The gap in his spirit left him helpless: neither alive with anticipation, nor dead from the exhaustion of the years of physical effort. What was he to do now?

He felt the pressure of not knowing, like the satchel at his ribs.

He reached the lane and looked down the shrouded avenue. No one. The children of the neighborhood had gone inside for dinner; the weather made it lonely.

He had wanted to be certain, but now he knew there would be no certainty. The terrible, pressing clarity of his vision did not permit certainty, though it demanded response. The closer he came the more he backed away.

And what would Hillary say when he told her that he had won?

Across the soft lawn, leaf-covered, shadowed by trees, he moved dreamlike toward the lighted windows of the patio porch. He sat and listened to the wind catching leaves and pulling them through air.

What was left? He got up and softly opened the sliding door to the living room. Without a sound he moved across the rug to the mantle and put the bird back in its place. Then he moved into the dining room across the creaking wooden floor.

"Mac?"

"It's me," McCallum said.

Hillary came out of the kitchen, trailing the sound of the television through the swinging door.

"You frightened me."

"The door was open," he answered, turning back toward the living room.

She gave him a kiss on the cheek. "How did it go? We missed the sports news."

"I lost."

She searched his face for a sign of disappointment, and he tried to continue the lie.

"It can't last forever."

The moment was broken by the children's shouting.

"Hi, Uncle Mac, did you win?"

"I won," he said.

He looked at Hillary, watching the veneer of her face crack.

"How high?" Marnie asked.

"Higher than I am. Way up here." He held his hand up for them to see.

"Can we see you in the next one?" John asked excitedly, starting to jump up and down in the dining room.

"You sure can."

Hillary turned away.

"You're the best then, Uncle Mac?"

"The best," he said, nodding.

"And you'll stay with us?"

He looked from John to Marnie, and then to Hillary, who stood near the wall without looking at him. "Sure," he said, "you know I will."

By the Way of Dispossession

To arrive where you are, to get from where you are not,
　You must go by a way wherein there is no ecstasy.
In order to arrive at what you do not know
　You must go by a way which is the way of ignorance.
In order to possess what you do not possess
　You must go by the way of dispossession.
In order to arrive at what you are not
　You must go through the way in which you are not.
And what you do not know is the only thing you know
And what you own is what you do not own
And where you are is where you are not.

　　　　　　　　　—T. S. Eliot, "East Coker," *Four Quartets*

One rule was to wait for the long ride; the other was to take anything going in your general direction. Sheppard thumbed moving backwards down the main street of Hays, Kansas. The passing cars dusted his clean, white shirt, but he smiled confidently with a closed-mouth grin that made him look younger than twenty-eight. Shaved clean, he knew that looking respectable was the quickest way to get a ride.

A car stopped, and Sheppard followed it, running awkwardly with his pack. He'd already decided which rule to follow.

"I'm not sure I'll be much help," the man said, leaning out through the open window. He took off his bow tie and opened his shirt collar. "I'm cutting off a little way up on U.S. 40 to Sharon Springs."

"I'll take wherever you're going," Sheppard answered.

He opened the back door, threw in his pack, and then climbed up front. On the way: it didn't matter about names. They were strangers and would always be strangers, but for reference and because the man asked, Sheppard gave an answer, a false one.

"You in school?" the man asked.

Questions equaled polite answers, not necessarily complete ones. "No, I finished school," Sheppard said. "I'm going home."

"Coming from where?"

"St. Louis. Been with a friend in St. Louis." True, but not quite true. He had also been other places.

The man told Sheppard he was from Sharon Springs. He'd been up to Hays to see about some shipments of feed and some tools that hadn't been delivered. Sheppard slid forward on the seat and leaned his head back to where he could just see over the dashboard to the highway shimmering in the heat. The land stretched out flat and dry.

"Haven't been to prison, have you?" the man asked, taking his foot off the accelerator and then trying to make the jerk of the car seem natural.

"No." Sheppard smiled at that.

"Not wanted?"

"Not even wanted." Truth: he had been to St. Louis to see his friend, Rehler. But before that was an immense time which seemed endless. He had been all the way from the mountains in Yugoslavia to the islands of Greece, then back up through Italy to the Camargue, and then up on the North Sea. Now he was going home.

He rested. Hot air blew through the car windows.

"You sleeping?" the man asked.

"Just thinking," Sheppard said. He watched the cornfields, the feed-lots, the land. Now and then he looked over at the man holding the Buick on the road. They seemed to ride on the noise of the motor. "How long you lived here?" Sheppard asked.

"All my life. Born over in Topeka though."

"Would you ever move away?"

"I got kids."

"I know." Sheppard pointed to the picture taped onto the dash-board: three kids. "But would you ever move away?"

"Where to?"

"I don't know. Anywhere."

"I might. If I found something better I might move away from what I've got."

"But you're not looking, are you?"

The man laughed. "Where'm I going to find something else? I got kids."

"What if I gave you some money to take care of your kids while you were looking for something else?" Sheppard suggested. "You do it?"

"You going to give me money?" Sheppard could see inside of the man's mouth.

"Let's just suppose."

"What do I do again?"

"You go looking for something else to do."

"Well, I'd have to get someone to do the business for me while I went. And someone to look after the animals and do the garden."

"That's all taken care of," Sheppard said.

"How?"

"Let's say that I do all that for you."

"Know how?"

"Nope, but let's say I do. I get help from one of the neighbors. Now where would you go looking?"

"Don't know yet," the man said. "I haven't thought about it. Too many problems to leaving though."

"We solved all those problems," Sheppard told him. "You and your kids and your wife got all the money you need. You got someone to take care of everything in case you want to come back. Everything will be just the same."

"Wouldn't be the same," the man said. "You can't expect that."

"Why not?"

"Changes every year. Sometimes it's hard to see."

"Let's say it doesn't change much."

"No, it doesn't change much anyway, whether we say it or not."

"Where would you start looking?"

The man tapped on the steering wheel. Sheppard let him have some quiet to think. The car slowed down.

"What's wrong?"

"This is where we turn to go down to Sharon Springs," the man said. He slowed way down and steered the car left. It seemed like a great effort. "Sure you want to go this way?"

"I'm sure I'll get there either way," Sheppard answered.

The car accelerated slowly, the sound of the moving air gathering at his arm in the window. Sheppard asked, "Think of anything yet?"

"No," the man said, smiling. "Haven't been putting a lot of mind to it though."

"Yeah, that's okay."

They drove in silence for the half hour into Sharon Springs. The ground was dry and dusty, the corn bleached out, hanging without moving in the air. In the clouds, a running dog and someone sleeping. Before the mountains are the plains. In the daytime the land stretches and rolls for hundreds of miles—part desert, part grassland—washed out and open. In a car you can drive an hour from anywhere and get water from rust-free pipes at a gas station or a restaurant. But the names of the towns still reflect the history of the land: River Bend, Rocky Ford, Springfield, Cheyenne Wells, Sharon Springs. Water, the life grace.

They pulled in slowly into the town. It was ninety-three degrees as they cruised up the main street.

"Maybe you'll get one of those air-conditioned cars," the man said.

"Maybe I won't get anything."

"You can take my map," the man said. "See where you are."

Sheppard nodded. The man pulled his car up to the curb, and Sheppard got out, pulling his pack with him.

"Good luck," the man said. They shook hands. "Truth is, I don't know where I'd begin to start looking for something else. I guess maybe Topeka, where I was born, but I don't like Topeka a lot. Don't matter much, because I can't leave here anyway."

Sheppard smiled with his lips closed together.

Heat rose off the dull breast of the country outside of Sharon Springs. At the edge of the land, moving toward Colorado, was the light-hot sky with its solid, rising clouds. It seemed a great distance in any direction.

Sheppard walked to the outskirts of town and sat down on the shoulder across from a gas station, not really hitching, but in sight. He folded out the beaten-up map.

Sweat dropping onto paper, he looked over the white space of Kansas, and then moved his hand west over the red and black highway lines. His mind seemed to slip over Highway 40 and the plains to the green patches of the mountains. He had been there before.

In St. Louis with Rehler, now a photographer, in the half-dark kitchen they had talked of all of that. Rehler had moved across the doorway, his hair silhouetted like a Medusa's head against the living room lights. "I always used to tell myself that it wasn't me," Sheppard said to him. "There I was in some remote place where I didn't belong, where no one belongs except the countrymen, and I would say to myself, 'Stay there,' because I *was* there. But at the same time I wasn't."

"How'd you find those places?"

"That's another thing. I don't know how I found them. I just heard about them from people I'd met, or I'd get there because I didn't care where I went."

Rehler had looked at him then and had suddenly hurried out of the room. A minute went by, and then the kitchen light snapped on like the sun, and Rehler was taking pictures of him. "Shut up," Rehler had shouted before Sheppard had moved, "Don't do anything!"

Later, at four in the morning, huddled in the reddish light of the darkroom, they developed the shots. Sheppard's face, absorbed in film, emerged onto the heavy paper.

"That doesn't prove anything," Sheppard protested.

"That's how you are. I swear to God."

"Come on." The pictures hung by clothespins on the wire. Rehler turned them so Sheppard could see. The lips were hard-set and tense and the eyes seemed blank. "I was just tired," Sheppard said.

Then a long pause, and Rehler said, "Why are you doing it?"

"There's no way to know why."

"There is," Rehler said. "Sit down and think about it. Don't drift. You've got money. You have everything you need."

Sheppard shook his head. "You know more than that," he said.

Across the highway a car pulled into the gas station. Colorado license. A travel-weary couple got out and went inside. The attendant got instructions and went to work wiping bugs off the windshield.

It would have been simple to go over and ask for a ride. They were going and it seemed as though they had enough room. But Sheppard hesitated.

Something else came to mind. He had wanted to stay away from home for a long time, and now he was going back. He had wanted to stay away from the things he knew, from questions, from *ease*. And yet always there was that vague sense of not being comfortable where he was. He had wanted to try living in many different places, and he had stayed in beach towns, in mountain villages, in cities. All he had with him was his pack—his clothes, a few small souvenirs—and yet he had many more things than he could carry on his back. He had rooms full of things stored at home, and anytime he wanted to he could have got the money to fly back. Always he said, "Stay there," wherever he was, but he knew, in the way that knowledge is sometimes hidden from consciousness, that his life was a simulation, an experiment. He found he loved life, but he couldn't stand it all the same.

And now, too, he didn't have to hitch. He could have taken a plane or a bus. But he had to create a difficulty, to put something into his path.

Across at the gas station, the couple got back into their car. The man exchanged words with his wife, and then, apparently satisfied that he was okay, motioned for Sheppard to come over for a ride. Sheppard waved back, pointing east: no thanks.

The car pulled out and headed west, its gears leveling out as it gathered speed. A new sense filled Sheppard then, as if he finally had something which he had to do. It would take a long time, and he did not know whether it would be possible. But he would try. The sure ride had faded into the blistering, wavy road. He had refused it, and now, swinging his pack over his shoulder, he started out to walk home across the plains.

Every day the sun cast its weight over the dry land. After the first afternoon he saw he would have to rise early to walk during the cooler morning, rest during the day's heavy heat, and then walk again in the evening. For the beginning, to see how it would be, he stayed along the highway, and in three days he had walked through Weskan, Arapahoe, and Cheyenne Wells.

He thought that at First View he would be able to see the mountains, but he reached the town in the heat of the day. The sun blurred the flat, baked land. There was a slow rise of land, a distant knoll, a few deep gullies where storm water had washed out the soil. Beyond the town, he saw a stand of cottonwoods in the distance, and he worked his way there to rest. There were no crops, no houses, no water. Only larks, and once in a while, a hawk circling, soaring, overhead.

When he stopped to rest, he propped up his pack and took out the photographs that Rehler had taken. He had packed them away at Rehler's insistence, "In case you want to look in a mirror," Rehler had said. Sheppard had not expected to look at them. The eyes disturbed him, because he wanted to see in them something that was not there. On film the eyes looked gray, tinged with the ambiguous character of his exhaustion.

He stood up in the hot shade of the cottonwoods. Despite the heat, he no longer felt like resting. Some things he did not like to think about.

"I just feel," Rehler had said, "that if you question everything, you have nowhere to stand."

"But I have to."

Rehler had pointed then to his camera, his darkroom with its trays and chemicals neatly arranged. "If I asked myself every day where I'm headed, I'd go crazy. I mean, sure, I may change, but at least I've got somewhere for the time being."

The next question, Sheppard knew: *and where have you got?* But instead, silence. Then Rehler asked, "Why are you going home so slowly?"

Time and again Sheppard stopped to check his progress over the white area of his map. He compared the quarter-inches on the map with looking up across the immense distances which separated him from the next rise of land. He began to see that the world was simple extension, that the map could not be real because it divided the land into parts. Land, like time, was unbroken. The land of the Indians was the same land as now, and all that the world had been in the past was a part of what it was now. He had never been in as strange a place as he was on the plains, on that desert east of the Colorado mountains.

At Kit Carson he ate a good meal, packed up from a grocery store as much as he could carry, and headed off in the evening toward Wild

Horse. There was a new coolness to the evening. Far to the west, where the mountains still lay invisible, the sun had already disappeared. The stars emerged in the dark blue sky, but far away west, clouds rose. Lightning: with each flash the clouds split apart into their layered formation, the lightning hesitating for a moment in the gray mist, and then racing through, gathering strength. There was no sound of thunder. The air hung still, the night furthering, and all that was left of the world in Sheppard's eyes was the general shape of the hills and the lightness of the ground.

He wasn't afraid. It seemed to settle his mind to be alone at night. That had always been so, too, wherever he was. Night prevented his being seen.

He wondered whether the movement of the storm would trouble him with rain. He thought of rain that he had known in the mountains, and he remembered the danger of drowning in a flash flood. The water cascaded down the mountains so quickly and forcefully that it could take you by complete surprise. He imagined himself now on the plains washed up on a sandbar, face into mud. Time distended, hours seemed to pass as he walked. He saw the face of someone with a loving smile. Face down on a sandbar, they would not know where to look for him.

The lights of the town came up far down the road. He felt strong now, and like going. At Wild Horse he wanted to leave the road and walk on a line across the land to the mountains.

Street lamps made the town seem even more deserted than it was. He felt self-conscious walking the street with his pack. His appearance had changed in the few days since Hays, Kansas. Now he no longer worried about his clean shirt or his unshaven face or the appearance of his smile—at least not for hitching. He felt tired, too, because he *was* tired.

He wanted to ask about the way just to be sure, and along the main street he finally found an old man sitting at an angle on a hard bench, a beer in his hand. Around his neck, hanging down onto a red shirt, was a leather string tie with a turquoise Indian stone in it. Behind him: a bar with the door open, talking and music.

The man spoke first. "Where are you coming from?"

"Just from Sharon Springs."

"Hitching?"

"Right."

The man looked him up and down, with the hint of a smile crossing a lined face. "Hasn't been a car through here for a half hour," the man said.

Sheppard smiled with his mouth closed. "I wanted to ask you something."

"Where you going?" the man interrupted.

"Colorado."

"You're in Colorado."

"The mountains, then," Sheppard said. "I used to live in Manitou."

The man sipped on his beer, shuffling a dirty pair of red and blue cowboy boots on the sidewalk, watching Sheppard and seeming to encompass all things at once. "You know these prairie storms?" he asked.

"No."

"Mountain storms and prairie storms aren't the same thing. Are you going on tonight?"

"If I can find out what it's like cutting across country from here."

The man looked at Sheppard again, as if weary of an idea he had heard too often. "Now there aren't no cars on that stretch ever."

Sheppard nodded, smiling again.

The man took out some tobacco and fitted some into his cheek. "Well, there's not so many fences as gullies. It would be quicker probably to take the road."

"You think?"

"Don't get caught in one of them gullies during the storm."

"Thanks." Sheppard nodded and moved away. He knew the same thing about mountain storms. Once down the road, he turned back and waved.

Outside of town Sheppard left the road to his right and started across unknown land. He knew he couldn't walk much farther in the night, but he wanted to get beyond the lights of Wild Horse so he could see the whole storm. For a half hour he continued, the sandy ground like a cover of snow. There was no real danger of getting lost or of falling into a gully. He could see straight out for a good half-mile.

He crossed several gullies, edging slowly down the steep, crumbling banks into the sandy bottoms, and then climbing up again to the flat earth on the other side. He wished he could sleep on the sand bottom of one of those gullies, that soft earth, but he knew that wasn't safe. Carefully he watched the flow of the lightning and felt the changes in the wind. Then, finally, on a bank overlooking a dry river, he decided that he would sleep as long as he could.

He laid out his sleeping bag in the dust. Then he cut some bread and cheese, and sat for a moment listening to the sounds. An owl cut through the air; the wind stirred the trees up the river; some small noises of scurrying animals; and in the distance the first rolls of thunder.

He awoke to a hard wind. Lightning flashed to the west, very close now, and the stars were gone. He packed up his bag and then sat down again to wait. There was no sense in moving.

The air filled with the smell of wet sage, and the night seemed to blacken before his eyes, though there was still no rain. Then suddenly, always surprisingly, the earth would appear before him for a shattering instant of time, revealing the strange desolation of a place of shadows and forms. Thunder rolled harder, seeming to close up the tear which only an instant before had allowed him to see through the world. He ran his hands through dust, not knowing how long he sat on the verge of that ecstasy.

Then the rain broke. It rolled across him like a part of the wind, the heavy drops leaving craters in the dust. Then the force of the whole storm was upon him, descending like some huge bird lunging. At first he put his face into it, feeling the wind and the sting of the rain. His hair matted and stuck to his neck and the water dripped inside his shirt. The dust and the sweat, which had been his for so many days, washed down, and he closed his eyes. For a long time he sat trance-like, wishing, though not at all afraid. He rubbed his hands in mud and washed them again in the air. Lightning flashed close by again, seeming to bring with it the hail.

And then the struggle: he covered his pack with his body. Everything he had was in it. He was so used to saying that, thinking it. He ducked his head as far down as he could, holding on. He could feel the painful blows of the hail on his back and arms. He tried to think, but the pain drove everything from him.

He did not know how long it lasted. It might have been momentary or a few hours. He lifted himself up, chilled and shaking, and brushed away the hailstones. The sand river was now a torrent of water, rising rapidly toward where he sat. But he did not move. The rain continued, soft now, gentle, moving on with the wind. The earth had turned wet and dark, and he could see nothing.

He waited. Though the storm had drifted east long ago, he had not tried to sleep. He had waited in one position, afraid to move. His arms and legs ached with the beating he had taken; his eyes burned sleepless with the thin light of the dawn. All the while he had seemed to be caught up in some thought, like a madman trying to grasp the one essential thing which troubled him.

The land awakened, emerged, oblivious to the terror. A lark flew on black and white wings and a light song. To the east, a fresh sky; west, darker, but now Sheppard could see the high, hard shape of the mountains. He walked until the sun was high up. His clothes dried quickly, but his boots were soaked through the leather and his pack was heavy. All the lightness, the confidence, with which he had started his walk had dissolved. Now he felt he had to keep moving all the time.

The gullies gave him more trouble. The banks now were slippery and several times he fell in the mud trying to hold his footing on the steep side walls. Climbing up and out was harder, too, and often he had to walk down the wet bottoms of the gullies to escape them. He wanted to hurry, and all detours made him more desperate.

In the early afternoon he was still moving. The air was muggy, hot, and he had not come upon any road. In the west the mountains had become clear, and he no longer consulted the map to measure his progress. He knew where he had to go but the distance seemed overwhelming, unchanging.

Toward mid-afternoon he saw an Indian knoll, a ceremonial hill rising high up out of the desolate flat land. He gauged himself by that, watching it grow larger as he approached. Finally he stood on the edge of a steep gully, the knoll just ahead, and watched a hawk circling easily in the air. It rose smoothly, never beating its wings, content to ride with the currents of the air.

Sheppard edged down the bank of the gully at last, trying to hold onto a sage plant for support. He found footholds, but the wall was steep and still muddy. At a solid-seeming point he let go from above, held fast for a second, and then jumped down into the wet sand. He tumbled over with the weight of his pack, and for a moment he lay there, his body relaxed, watching the hawk soaring in the blue sky. He closed his eyes.

An instant later, a gunshot. He jerked up, startled, just catching a glimpse of the hawk fluttering out of the sky.

Sheppard was up immediately and started to climb the west side of the gully, slipping and clawing his way up. At the rim he saw the hawk on the ground, flapping one wing. The other wing was extended uselessly. A shrill cry broke the silence.

Over the rim, Sheppard went running, the pack bouncing on his back. He threw it down before he reached the bird. Another shot rang, and the hawk's body bounced and feathers splattered into the air. Sheppard stopped and everything was quiet again.

For a long moment he hesitated, looking at the crumpled bird. He wavered, feeling the heat, the energy rising in him again, and then he ran forward and grabbed the bird and raced back toward the protection of the gully. The moments hung. His legs hurt, dragging the heavy boots over the few yards. But the next shot came too late as he dived over the rim and skidded down the embankment.

Quickly he was up again, still holding the bird. His hands were bloody, and the redness stained his white shirt as he carried the bird close against his chest. His arm was wrenched from the fall, but he scrambled along the bottom of the gully, finding an off-shoot where he cautiously climbed the lower part of the wall to look out.

He saw no one. At least no one was coming down for him yet. He tried to make out where the shots had come from, and the only likely place was the knoll. He watched this spot for a while, but nothing moved. His mind raced, not understanding anything.

He held the bird out away by a talon and looked at it. One wing hung loosely, bloodied by the first shot; the other curved gently back into its juncture with the body, which had been torn apart by the second bullet. The red-orange tail was muddy and spattered with blood.

Then Sheppard looked back out to the land and saw his pack where he had thrown it onto the ground. All his things—his sleeping bag, his food, the photographs—were in it. But he had nowhere to hide. If the shooter wanted him he could have his clear shot if Sheppard went after the pack.

Then something else passed through his mind. Sheppard smiled grimly. The pack was no longer his. It belonged to the shooter, and the bird belonged to him.

He looked out again to see the shooter emerge from behind the rocks. He came slowly off the hill, carrying the rifle in two hands in front of him.

Sheppard turned quickly and moved back into the main stream of the gully. There would be a short time when the shooter could not see him in the bottom, when his vision would be blocked out. Without the pack he could run. That was important now to life, to staying alive. And if the man stopped for the pack, Sheppard knew the shooter would never catch him. So Sheppard ran. With labored steps along the soft sand, clutching the hawk under his arm, he ceased to care about what was behind him.

The Clay Urn

A drop hits the bottom of the clay urn which is flesh, and from the moment of birth, drop by drop, the pain begins to fill us. That was why Nate always thought the best life was the one which expired one second after it began, after the first touching drop. A cry and a slap and then death—the body only, and the smallest of spirits, unable to reflect, knowing no pain, not waiting one's life until the urn overflowed.

What then? Only a name.

Nate Rose watched as they lowered the child's casket into the earth's scar, the brown hole they had dug in the white winter ground. This child was eight. Nate thought the child had lived too long.

It was the child of the woman who had once been to Nate as name-less as he was now to her. She was dressed simply in a heavy brown coat against the cold and a black hat pulled down over her dark hair. She held her head down, watching the descending casket, and perhaps praying with her tears.

He stood opposite her in the crowd, so that he could see her well. A minister stood nearby reciting, and around her: friends, family— people Nate had seen before in the neighborhood, some he had never seen, all of whom he did not know. He imagined them as the woman's father and mother, her brother, aunt, brother's wife. He saw no father of the child. No more, though he saw the apparition of a husband and a father, one father who art in heaven. No, Nate thought. *Our.*

Was this the reason he had come now? To watch the woman's face ringed with sleepless black marks? Lonely sleepless black marks. He added that much in his consciousness: lonely. Lonely as in his mirror.

Child to whom he once spoke: It was November, late in the month. Nate had been walking in the dust, past the shouts of the schoolyard, when Charles had emerged, laughing, with a friend. He had watched them before, watched Charles before, knowing it was the woman's boy. Then he had not known names. The boy's world, the idols and lazy running, excited running, games built from air and television and sports. Life of the home, life without thought when you are eight. As if drawn by gravity at that age, accepting punishment and love equally and never doubting, never thinking of doubting, never thinking at all, yet still unconsciously breaking away, trying to break away from the gravity which drew you homeward.

Leaving his friend, the boy walked in Nate's direction, toward their separate houses, but along the same street.

Nate tossed a football with him. Even in his inexperience Nate thought his age would make him capable. But the child threw better than he. They traded tosses from the sidewalk to the middle of the street where the child walked.

"Who is your favorite player?" Nate asked first.

"Kenny Houston," Charles had said, giving the football a little sting. "He plays defense though."

Nate did not compound his inability with his ignorance. "Do you have a team of your own?"

"We're too little for a real team. But later."

Nate remembered the later. Later for games. "What does your father do?" he had asked.

Not knowing, just beginning then to watch the boy's mother as she stretched in her back yard to hang clothes. He might have told from the clothes she hung that there was no father, but he had not noticed it till later. He had watched only her: the stirring of her legs, reaching, her breasts outlined against a work blouse, her hair hanging loosely without thought or care. He watched from his window two houses down, over two fences, seeing more than he could really see with his eyes.

The child had looked at him while the question was loose in the air. A child holding a football in his hand ready to throw and then deciding not to throw. "I just live with my mother," he had said.

The boy said the words so naturally that no other words seemed necessary. But there was a shortness in the words so that Nate was able to see the drops falling slowly into the urn. He saw at that moment the mother in the child, the set line of the lip which told Nate there was a duty even in a child which must be carried out before all other things— a duty to keep silent and to continue.

The child's resolution had drawn Nate in, had made him love. Love tinged with fright.

The little long-haired child began to throw the football into the air, spinning it laterally and then catching it himself, as if he were catching all the world.

It was the child, not the woman, who first noticed Nate. "You're around a lot," Charles said. "I see you places all the time."

Nate remembered these words had warmed him, though the child had said them as fact, as time-chasers.

"Where do you see me around?"

"I don't know where," Charles said. "Just around on the street and places."

They had reached the woman's house. There had been a pausing but no goodbye.

Not even a where-do-you-live from the child. Just a small room on the second floor. Two houses down at Mrs. Donahue's. Nate had smiled.

His first days there had been numb; Nate remembered nothing of them. He had had no habits, knew nothing of the stores, or where to buy the things he needed. He had brought nothing with him. He had cared about nothing. Gradually he had begun to notice the walls, his street, even Mrs. Donahue, whom he saw every day. Then he had seen the other houses, the trees, and the rolling hills.

At first he had watched Mrs. Grace with a kind of detachment, the way one might watch a cloud crossing the sky—a cloud without meaning except in its being the only cloud crossing the sky; that was its meaning. And he saw her child, Charles, though he watched Charles without so much detachment because Charles had the same face as she and had what Nate imagined her smile to be if she had ever smiled at him.

And then two months later. Later, now.

Charles disappeared under the earth, the minister said some further words, and the mother continued her stolid, silent crying with her mouth set. The mother crying watching knowing that this moment was the disappearance. Nate thought: though she cannot see him even now, she knows he is in there. The lid is closed. Soon there will be shoveling and worms.

The minister finished his words and the people began to move away. The woman stayed; Nate stayed. The people walked back toward the parked cars along the stepped-out path in the snow.

As though it had meant nothing to them.

Everyone had been polite to leave her alone except Nate. He could not have moved away with them.

The minister saw him and came over, touched Nate on the arm. "Leave the woman in peace now," he said softly.

Nate looked at the man, knowing the minister would make no scene over his staying. The minister tried persuading with his eyes, but Nate bound himself, feet upon the earth, to Mrs. Grace. When the minister had turned away, she looked up at him—an instant—must have seen him, he thought, before she turned her head downward once more.

Or was she, as he later thought, her pure mother's love? Was she her own love and nothing else, the way some men are only their passions? The mother bound by the indefinable cord of attachment. The object deceased, the love existing, though now unattached to anything real: *she* unattached, but her love welling up. The way Nate had only his thoughts and his imagination. The same imagination which, after his meeting with the child, simultaneously saw the child playing in the schoolyard and the mother hanging the clothes he wore; which saw the child throwing the ball and laughing and her joy in him as he ran to her in the yard; which saw the child's running and the mother's movements, slow and tentative, as she walked in her small garden. The imagination which said to Nate: "If the child knew this much pain from the father, then the mother must know all the child's and her own, too." As Nate himself, having lived for thirty-two years would someday die too late, filled up and overflowing.

Nate thought often about loving her. Knowing she was alone in the house all day without the child. Not loving her as a mistress, no. But just *once,* skin against skin touching. And then see. Just one night to prove finally that even the things he knew were farthest from him were flesh.

When Nate contemplated her position after the funeral, he knew she must move away. Whether she saw him or not with that one look, she must move away, because she had a family and friends to go to for comfort and for talk and to take her mind away from being alone. Although they cannot ever keep her from being alone now, Nate thought. Only he could do that.

Two days later, she left with a small suitcase, her family by her side. She walked slowly, almost led by them, with her head still down. The family's car, not her own, took her away.

In her absence Nate watched the house. Weeks passed. No change. No "For Sale" sign on the lawn. He knew she was coming back.

The same car brought her.

Now she moved as though her life were over, and it did not matter to her where she lived the rest of it. Except, he thought, she didn't know about him.

Of all the friends Nate had had before (he could have named names but there was no point), he realized: his life spanned and encompassed all of their lives, all their desires and needs, and stretched beyond them to self-seeking. Now he saw the length and breadth of a rising and falling sea upon which he sailed, conscious of the sailing, but more aware of the sea. It was not the boat but the sea he cared for: the sea composed of drops in which the world would drown; the sea, like the mother's love, made from his imagination; the sea, thin and vaporous, composed of all the impossibilities which lay before him.

Nate saw the woman often. One day in February, during a warm lull in the winter, he watched her leave with her shopping basket and walk toward the market where she shopped. He followed just to be close, watching her soft walk and her shoulders moving beneath a light coat. He did not know why he kept so far behind, trying not to be seen. She did not know him. In the market aisle she passed him as if he were not there at all.

He observed everything new about her. Her eyes had lost some of their shimmer since the boy had died, but that loss only made them seem deeper. Her face seemed older in misery than it had in happiness. The hair, before neglected and matted, now had a tentative, cared-for look, not to make herself attractive, but to spend time in curling and combing. Otherwise she was the same: powderless face, proper and fashionless clothes.

He knew what she was going through, knew exactly what her life was to her, drop by drop.

which was why he thought of her, why he found himself bound up with her life.

why as her arm passed close to him in the market he imagined stroking her arm and lying beside her in her empty bed.

with consent, all without words but with consent, the consent of a look and a movement of the hand which would say to him yes.

To always feel constant—not happy—but constant and the same. Nate wished for that. He could live with pain so long as it remained the same magnitude. He had lived for years with an ache in his arm, but it was always the same ache, and he knew it was there. If the pain becomes less then one begins to hope, and if it becomes greater one despairs. And Nate Rose, as the days went by watching Mrs. Grace, knew that the urn was slowly filling, coming closer to the top.

The child, forgotten now, under the earth. Days went into spring, longer slower days. Nate spent much of his time in his room. Sometimes he wrote letters to the past, but he never mailed them. The only person with whom he spoke was Mrs. Donahue, who stopped him on the stairs nearly every day.

"Do you have everything you need, Mr. Rose?" she called out from the kitchen.

"Yes, thank you," Nate said. Usually he hurried off. He never had anything to ask.

Several times he had gone to visit the tiny grave to see whether there were any change in it. A small stone inscribed "Charles Grace," without dates, as if he had been as old as they; as if he had lived and grown full as they would; as if the name alone were enough to say what needed to be said. *No one knew anyway.*

Except the mother and Nate.

The distance between them expanded with the passing time, diminished by his imagination. Nate had still not brought himself to speak with her.

One cold morning—foggy, so he could barely see over to her house—Nate watched Mrs. Grace come out. She got into the car. Nate could hear the motor turning but not catching, and then he imagined the smell of too much gasoline. Mrs. Grace got out and looked under the hood as if she could locate the source. Then she tried again. Nate sat with sweated hands, got up and opened the window, then closed it again suddenly, almost with a slam.

He had learned cars inside out. But he waited and watched as she went back inside, as the service man finally came, a man in a clean white suit this morning. The man spent fifteen minutes fiddling until the motor finally caught and idled.

All the space of the sea lay before him. His action never coincided with what he had been taught or with what he wanted. He desired peace and he desired disruption: love and distance simultaneously, security and freedom, conformity and individuality, joy and pain.

He walked the room in circles several times. When he went to the window again, the service man and Mrs. Grace were both gone.

Days of spring moved into days of summer. Days burned and the nights enveloped the house in a swarthy moist darkness. Children played outdoors until dark, and then barbecue smoke hung in the air with smells of chicken and steaks. Laughter, music; cars raced by. The neighbors sat outside in the warm air. Nate often walked in the dark past the woman's house. He never saw her sitting outside to watch the others; she never took part; and he never saw her at the window.

It was on these summer walks that Nate's mind began turning and changing. He expected courage of himself every time he saw her during the day, and yet by night she was as far away from him as a ghost boat upon the sea. All the space of the sea opened out before him. He watched it rise and fall across the horizons, wishing that it would stay the same. But once thinking began, the sea rose up and out beyond him, it seemed to go on and on and never to end.

As the sea rolled at night, so during the day Nate made resolutions. He wanted to learn every detail of her life. He circulated among the store owners of the neighborhood, asking.

"Do you know Mrs. Grace? How much do you know?" He was speaking to the hardware man.

"Mrs. Grace?" Mr. Gill answered. "Is she the one who lost the child? Yes, I've seen her, but not very much. She shops over in Tracy's market. What was the disease the child had?"

"That's the woman," Nate said. "The child had pneumonia. But what do you know of her?"

"Nothing."

But he did not go to Tracy's. He went to the flower shop and talked to the owner. "She's never ordered flowers from me," the woman said. I know the one you mean though. Quiet one."

"That's right. Do you know anything about her husband?" Nate asked.

"Never saw him. Why do you want to know all this?" The woman looked at Nate suspiciously. "What has she done?"

"Nothing, just curious."

He did not ask at Tracy's, or at the bank, or at the service station which had come when her car broke down; nor did he talk with Mrs. Donahue or any of the neighbors. He asked only where no one knew anything about her.

He intended no harm. Always he expected that he would say something to her or help her in some small way: to carry her packages, to open her car door, to save her from some accident, to escort her.

Each time she came near to him he backed away. Quiet. She looked away and did not see him. She busied herself sorting vegetables; or when she drove by slowly in her car, it was as if he had been soaked up by the heat of the pavement.

She could not have failed to see him, he thought. She pretended.

It did not cross his mind that he bothered her. How could he if she did not see him? Nor did he think he acted strangely. His loneliness eased when he watched her.

One day he watched her carry on a long, animated conversation with the neighbor who lived between their two houses, a Mrs. Lapin. The two women stood at the fence for over an hour in the sun, their voices carrying all the way to the open window where he sat. He could not hear them clearly. Mrs. Grace would bend down to her gardening and continue talking and then straighten up again and point out something in the garden. Occasionally Mrs. Grace would look right at him, as if she knew exactly where his window was and what he was doing there and what he felt sitting there. But she never pointed to him and asked Mrs. Lapin; she never seemed really to see him; she never made a sign.

Nate wondered. Certainly there were people on the street that he did not notice. He saw them as he saw parking meters or lamp posts. But that was in cities where people were a horde. And even then a woman might catch his attention one day, and he would remember her the next. Or a man with a good-smelling pipe, or another on crutches. He would remember them. In a small neighborhood where the daily lives were so close, where the same people shopped in the same stores, he would not have avoided noticing the familiar faces. He remembered the supermarket check-out girl when he saw her at the movies with her boyfriend, and he recognized the service station man when he watched his son play ball at the field. And so on. He noticed, and he knew she could not help noticing either.

Nate often wondered whether the boy had recounted anything of their meeting. Perhaps the boy had mentioned that a man had asked about the father. But the woman had given no sign. There had been nothing, either before the death or after it, which answered him.

Make himself known. Over and over he thought of the simple device of conversation. If she talked so long to Mrs. Lapin, wouldn't she do the same with him? Or couldn't he engage Mrs. Lapin in talk, ask her for something just at the moment when Mrs. Grace was there at the fence? Or more directly, simply go to Mrs. Grace's door and greet her?

But Nate could do none of these things. It gradually dawned on him that he did not want to meet her. He could not go to Mrs. Lapin to ask, just as he could not go to help with her car, or carry her groceries. He did not want to know anything about her which would destroy her.

Toward the end of the summer: another season was coming. One day his landlady, Mrs. Donahue, approached him about the lease for the coming year. She questioned him about the renewal and he seemed far away. He heard her questions without seeing he had to answer them, without knowing the questions had something to do with where he was and whether he could go on living there. It was as if he did not know her, whom he saw everyday.

"Well, Mr. Rose," she said. "You don't have to tell me right now, of course. I can wait one or two weeks if you want to make up your mind in private. I know you are a very private person, Mr. Rose, and I wouldn't want to disturb you." Then she paused and looked at him. "Can I ask you something else?"

She waited for an answer, but he gave none.

She continued, "Where do you come from, Mr. Rose? Don't you have any family? And what do you do all day? You don't have to work, I assume. I'm not complaining because you always pay me right on time. I suppose you have money. But are you going to do this forever?"

She looked at him quizzically.

He did not answer. Instead, he turned and walked up the stairs to his room, the question remaining like frozen words. He saw them written on the child's stone.

Days went on. He thought of her totally, dreamed of her body against his, envisaged her child Charles, and then another child like Charles but also like himself. He imagined her former husband, what he might have looked like, how the other man might have attracted her. But when he imagined the husband, he had no image, the way a man's name like Jesus' cast an image upon him by itself. He simply saw Mr. Grace as nothing but having been. He saw the man killed in a plane crash, dead of a heart attack, shot in the war, murdered. Or had he merely disappeared? Into prison? In the war? Deserted her and not returned? And then, would he come back?

Was that what she was waiting for?

Absorption, and little by little, the drops of the sea fell into the urn, pushing air into the remainder of the air, the larger air. Gradually over months of watching her, the urn had filled.

He saw his whole life, future life, passing before him in this anonymous pursuit, a compulsion never changing. As his money dwindled away to nothing, as she aged and died, as he aged and died, it remained the same. Or, as she moved away, unaware even that she was leaving him behind, it was the same. Even when such thoughts came to him and he resolved faithfully to go to her, he knew the resolve would fade away with the day, merely becoming more drops and more,

until before him the sea lay in her form, the trackless endless mystifying core which had become now, in the full urn, his total life. All else was now pressed outward and he saw only her, did everything—which was as nearly nothing as a man can do—only for her. He wished to know all of her and nothing; all he wished was at the end, a touch. For that he did not hope. He saw before him the life of questions—*are you going to do this forever?*—but it no longer mattered to him. The urn had filled, until the day came, just as the day had come when he had left his old life. The pain had changed. He had despaired of the poor child who died too late and he walked down the street past Mrs. Lapin who said a cheery good afternoon to him and he walked right up to the woman's door and rang the bell of her house. He did not know what he was doing, the thought flashing through his mind that he was killing himself as surely as if he were putting a gun to his head, and she opened the door and stood there before him with half-cared-for hair and a strange silent expression which she had carried on her lips for as many months as her child was dead and she said to him, with a faint smile,

"Hello, Mr. Rose. Won't you come in?" as though she had been expecting his coming for a long time.

The Humpbacked Bird

The shadow of the vulture drifted across the rocky hill in front of them, and the two men stopped and looked up. Schafer raised his hand to block the midday glare of the sun and squinted to find the bird that belonged to the shadow.

"Alone," Tom said of the vulture. He took off his wide-brimmed hat and, with a bandana taken from the pocket of his red shirt, he wiped his face clean of sweat. "From the way he's soaring, he hasn't found anything yet."

Schafer trained the binoculars on the bird, picking out the feather-less, pink head and the way, unlike a hawk, the vulture's wings tilted upward as it spiraled on the high currents of air. "Could sure as hell see the boy from up there."

"Not if the boy's under cover where he should be. Everything alive had better be in the shade."

It had not rained in that part of the country in six months. Across the wide stretch of desert, they could see the dark clusters of rocks in the Christmas Mountains and the many gullies where the land had been washed. At noon the mountains and the gullies were without the definition of shadow, treeless, and baked dry.

"That's the trouble with searching," Tom went on. "You have no-where to start."

Schafer let his pack slide down into the hooks of his elbows, glad to ease the rubbing of the straps on his shoulders. "If I were that kid," he said, "I'd try to head for the river."

Tom tied the bandana around his forehead and settled the hat back onto his head. He was a lean man with dusty red hair, and he looked as though he had been born to that dry, desolate country of West Texas. His features were stark, like yucca thorns, and he seemed to have the nervous quickness that animals require for survival.

Schafer looked at Tom with a certain envy. Having drifted south from Colorado, Schafer was not used to the heat or to the rugged country of the Sierra del Carmen. Tom seemed hard to him, but Schafer often thought it was that he was so soft himself. He envied Tom his indifference.

They watched the vulture ride high up, and when it was nearly out of sight over the crest of the hill ahead of them, Tom started up again toward the ridge. For half an hour Schafer labored to find a rhythm to his stride that would make it easier. But he kept thinking of the boy. Except for the Rio Grande fifteen miles away, there was no water. The alkaline stream beds were crusted white, and the whole country was bleached out and scorched by the heat.

They had never met Joel. At the ranch where they worked, Tom had been ordered out onto the search because he knew the country better than anyone else. Tom had argued that it was impossible to go in and find someone unless you knew him. "You can track a deer," Tom had said, "but not a stranger."

"Trying is better than sitting and waiting," Schafer had countered. "Think of him out there."

"Then you come with me."

Schafer had volunteered, though he did not know very much about the desert. All he knew was that the boy's parents had been exploring the old wax camp roads when the boy had suddenly told them to stop the car. There had been some sort of fight, and Joel had opened the door and run. He was fifteen.

"And we're asked to believe that?" Tom had said when he had heard the story.

"What difference does it make what we're told?" Schafer had asked. "All we have to do is find him."

"If he wants to come out, he'll come out."

"He's *lost*," Schafer had said, almost angry at Tom.

Tom had shaken his head. "You have to learn to take care of yourself," Tom had said. "I had to learn, too. But I guess I don't have much choice about going."

Now before them was the wild Sierra del Carmen and the Deadhorse Mountains, a land so barren that only a few stands of juniper and piñon were hardy enough to color the side of one high mountain.

A jagged ridge of rock broke the white-hot skyline in the distance ahead of them, and they both understood that the land did not stop there. Beyond the first canyon below them was the ridge, and beyond that, another canyon and a continuation of the scarred, serrated hills which seemed endless.

Schafer had come slowly across the arid region, moving a little farther south each year, as though he found it necessary to sink to the bottom of the map. For a while he had worked as a mechanic in Sanderson, where Alene had grown up. Knowing no one, his life was putting in hours at the shop and frequenting the billiard hall or a movie. It had been, really, no different in any other town or city from Colorado on down. Farmington, Albuquerque, Alamogordo, El Paso. After a few months he had felt burned out, not from the dry heat, but from a feeling that he was doing nothing. He wanted to change that.

Once in a while in Sanderson he would see Alene next door. Though he guessed she was between twenty and twenty-five, she seemed to him older. Her hair was streaked, but dull and uncared for, and she walked with the slow, uneven stride of an old person. Once or twice he had tried to speak to her, but each time, for some incalculable reason, he felt himself turn shy, withdrawn, as though he were afraid of her. From her going and coming, he figured she must have worked in town, but when he looked for her at lunch or after work, he seldom saw her on the street. It was just at home that he saw her, next door where she lived with her parents. By saying hello over the fence, he could make her smile, but he noticed too that the smile never reached her eyes.

One evening, looking out from the window of his basement apartment where he was cooking supper, he saw her in the window across the way. She seemed to be studying him, though she gave no sign. And from that day on, he left the curtains open day and night so that she could see everything he did. He was too shy to go to her, and he began to dream that some night she would knock on his door and ask. Like many men who had nothing, it was easy to make his whole life hinge upon a woman he had never met.

In the spring, one night after a movie they crossed paths coming up the aisle. "Are you walking home?" he asked.

She smiled briefly and nodded, and he went along with her on the sidewalk. She was not as attractive as he had imagined, and yet he barely noticed the ungainly way she moved or the sallow skin of her arms in the street light.

"There's the train," she said.

He heard nothing except the crickets.

"You can feel it in the ground," she said.

In a moment the whistle of the train sounded behind the hill, and the beam of the engine's light funneled down through the darkness outside of town. He never noticed the slight shake of the ground until the train was almost even with them.

At the juncture of their sidewalks, when he was making up words in his mind to say good night, she kept walking toward his basement apartment, just as though he had asked her. She waited for him at the door.

"I didn't expect you to visit," he said, holding the door for her. "I haven't cleaned up."

He stood back and let her pass, following her into the room. The dank smell of his dirty, oily clothes had collected in the shut-up space, and he stood for a moment by the door while she moved through the room in the dark.

"Don't turn on the lights," she said, turning back suddenly.

Then she went on across the room to the windows. "We don't need the curtains open anymore either," she said, pulling them across and closing the room away from the street lamps outside. She turned toward him and smiled.

There was a brazenness about her in that moment, born more from her apparent resolution to carry the act through to the end than from any real feeling. To him she looked nervous as she took a couple of steps toward him. "Well?"

He looked at her full for the first time, waiting. "Are you sure?" he asked.

"Yes."

Schafer felt the heat and the dampness rise to his face. He cared too much to refuse, and yet he knew right away she was pretending. So he let her begin.

"People have looked away from me all my life just as though I were invisible," she said. "But you're not looking away."

"I want to see you."

"I'm afraid to let you."

Then, feigning boldness of his own, he went to her. Most of his experience had been lonely encounters with women to whom nothing mattered, and he was awkward in trying to caress Alene softly. But in that room with the curtains drawn, she did not see his imperfections, nor he hers. With sighs and touches, the helpless, self-consciousness they each hated in themselves dissipated, and they undressed and walked to the unmade bed.

It was over in what seemed like an instant, coupling briefly and then ebbing. The silence gathered between them once again. He edged away from her and hid his face in the warm spot of her neck where he held his breath. He expected her to cry then, but she lay looking up at the ceiling for a long time, her left arm draped over him without pressure, her right hand rubbing her stomach and thighs, as though proving to herself that what had happened had been true.

"Are you cold?" he asked.

"No, I'd better go."

She started to get up, but he held her down gently.

"Please," she said. She got up and moved across the room on bare feet to gather her clothes.

"Are you all right?"

"Yes."

"I'd rather have you stay."

She did not answer, but instead began dressing, as though she had been through that ritual of going home a hundred times.

"Are you angry? You. . . ."

"I'm not angry," she said quietly. "I'll be back another time."

He looked at her across the dark room. He had not known then the depth of her moods and silences, though later he would learn about them. He had the feeling that she was more afraid than he was, and that she knew by leaving she could avoid all questions.

Schafer called the boy's name twice and then waited.

"Joel! Joel!"

The sound died out in the hot, motionless air without an echo. Heat waves rising from the ground blurred the rocky hillside in front of them, and Schafer felt his shirt sticking to his skin.

"It won't do any good to call," Tom said.

"What do you think we should do?"

Tom looked carefully down the empty draw toward the river. The canyon ran north and south and was strewn on both sides with heavy boulders which had fallen from the rim and had rolled part of the way down. "There's a lot of hiding room here," he said. "A lot of shade. If we have to do anything, I guess we should each take a side of the canyon and head up toward the mountain."

"You don't think we should head down?" Schafer asked, looking south where the canyon walls bent and closed off the way to the river.

"I don't think he would know there was a river here," Tom said coldly. "We can camp on the mountain where it's cool, and maybe he'll be able to see a fire and come to us."

Schafer took a swallow from his canteen, washed his mouth, and spat out the warm water onto the ground. The boy had already spent one night out in that wasteland, and Schafer hoped he would not have to go through another.

"I'll flip you for sides," Tom said, drawing a half from his jeans pocket. He spun the coin high into the air.

"Heads."

Tom caught the half and slapped it over on his wrist. "Always call tails," he said before he looked at the coin. He smiled and lifted his hand. "Tails. I'll take this side. You go across."

Schafer shrugged his shoulders. "I knew it beforehand," he said, gathering up his pack. He stood for a moment on the west rim looking at the distance he had to climb. He had to go down into the canyon, across the sand river, and then out again to the east rim.

"Are you up to it?" Tom asked.

"I'll make it." Schafer studied Tom's bony face. "Let's take it slowly for the boy's sake."

"We aren't going to find him," Tom said, "take it slow or not. We just have to finish up what we started."

An hour later, as he looked out from the east rim, the Sierra del Carmen sifted toward orange and red in the afternoon light. Schafer scanned the area with the binoculars, crossing gullies and hills and draws slowly. He picked up nothing. The lifeless, inert land bulged in the circle of his wide-angle glasses, and he wondered what had made Joel pick this place to run away.

He lowered the binoculars and turned around. The sun had edged outward, as though travelling a line rather than an ellipse, and the west rim was iced in shadow. Tom was merely a red swath of shirt, recognizable only by color and movement against the backdrop of the Christmas Mountains as he hiked the ridge. He ought to have been down below the rim in the rocks, Schafer thought, where he could look into the caves and crevices. It would take longer and it would be tougher to move, but they weren't out there to make it easy on themselves.

When he had caught his breath, Schafer moved off the rim, still calling the boy's name even though the sound did not carry. In the dead heat of the afternoon he crawled through the narrow passages between the rocks, shouting to Joel until, with the repetition, the name began to sound unreal to him. His voice cracked, and he felt as though he were mouthing a child's meaningless song. "Joel, Joel, Jol, Jal, Jo-el." He began to lose the sense of where he was.

Headed toward the point of the triangle where the canyon closed into the side of the mountain, he could have been in any state, in any country. He was working harder than he had ever worked in his life and was getting nowhere. Neither an answer from Joel, nor a sign. But he could not stop. He checked across the canyon again for Tom.

Several minutes before, Tom had been far ahead of him in an open spot on the rim near a high rock formation. Now, at first glance, Schafer did not see him. Schafer climbed to the top of a rock and brought up the glasses.

He moved the circle of the glasses along the west rim, passing the rock formation and then coming back to it, thinking that Tom had simply been cut off from view. The formation looked like a huge humpbacked bird, the angle of two separate rocks forming wings upraised and a lump of limestone on its back pinning the bird to the ground. Schafer stared, imagining the bird's span of centuries, hearing the night sounds, feeling the pull of winds and the wash of rain. The weight of limestone had held it there like a prisoner's chain.

The red shirt did not emerge. Schafer waited a few minutes and rested. Then he thought that perhaps Tom had found the boy. He tried to call across, but the new sound of Tom's name evaporated as soon as it left his lips. A kind of panic began to fill him. Tom had found the boy, and Schafer wasn't able to do anything, wasn't able to help. It was too steep to climb down at that point, and instead, he climbed back out to the east rim. He started running.

The pack bounced crazily on his back, throwing him off stride, and in a few minutes he stopped, realizing he was making no progress. Across the canyon the humpbacked bird had now changed form, and the wings of the bird had now become the ears of some wolflike animal. Two great black holes made the pockets for eyes which seemed to stare out at him. Then from behind those eyes, he saw Tom starting to climb back up to the west rim.

Alene had been happy when they were ready to move down to the trailer on the ranch. In the few months they'd known each other, she had changed noticeably. Though she could never make herself truly pretty, the brighter dresses she wore and the curled hair and make-up gave her the appearance of being new. Her parents were pleased, and their original suspicion of Schafer when he'd asked to marry her had altered into a warm feeling of gratitude.

"She hasn't ever had the kind of attention that a woman needs," her father told Schafer one night on the porch.

"Well, she'll get it now," Schafer assured him. "I hope she'll do as well on the ranch as she's done here."

Alene had come out onto the porch. "Why shouldn't I?"

"It'll be hot and dry and fewer people," he told her. "I don't know whether I can take it myself."

She smiled. "I'd rather be around fewer people."

Schafer was as worried about himself as he was about her. It was as though he had come to the border now and had exhausted all other options. But he had a great deal of hope. Alene had made the difference to him, had made him see that he could hang on if he really wanted to, and he was determined that this job would be for a long time.

And Alene had done well. Schafer made the effort to compliment her often, whether on her cooking or her appearance or her lovemaking, and she responded with a willingness to try to break from her old habits even more profoundly. She was more talkative, seemingly more open. Yet he still did not understand her moods.

Sometimes she seemed to escape into some dream, as though she interrupted what she was doing, becoming more lonely when she was with him than when she was alone. He did not expect to know everything about her, and yet he wanted her to feel that he cared to know if she would tell him.

Several months after they had settled into the trailer, he caught her in a mood. He had cleared away the supper dishes while she was sitting over a cup of coffee, and he turned to find her far away.

"What's wrong?"

"Nothing." She broke the dream and turned to him with a smile.

"What were you thinking then, just now, with your eyes open?"

"Remembering," she said.

"What?"

She got up from the table. "All the things you don't know about me."

"I want to know them," he said. "But it doesn't matter if I don't."

"Don't even imagine." She went over to the sink and stood looking out the window into the yard, where at night a fluorescent light made the hard ground seem like an empty ball field. "I hate vultures," she said. "They barely even eat."

"What are you talking about?" He conjured up the image of the huge black birds that stalked the yard during the day and scavenged at the ranch dump. He looked out his separate window from the sofa. "There aren't any vultures out at night."

"You don't see them."

Beside the trailer in the men's bunkhouse, a clatter caught their attention and a door banged hard. Tom Bailey came out and started across the yard toward the barns on the other side.

"Did you know Tom is from Sanderson?" she asked.

"No." He watched Tom stop in the center of the yard and light a cigarette.

"He was older than I was, but in school he was quite a football player."

"That must have been a while ago," Schafer said. "He doesn't look now as though he ever did much except work with cattle."

"He was a kind person," she said almost wistfully. She looked back toward the sofa, not seeing Schafer directly, but staring at some point distant which only she could see. He did not like those silences of hers for they gave him nowhere to go. Finally she asked, "Do you think I'm afraid?"

"Afraid of what?"

"I don't know." She paused a moment to think. "Afraid of things generally."

"You mean like vultures?"

She didn't answer, but looked out into the yard. "It's only that I've always felt until now that there was nothing I could lose."

"What can you lose now?"

"You."

He did not understand that then, but he knew the kind of desperation that was in her voice. It was that emptiness that lonely people sensed when they had no one to whom they could turn for help. He stood up and smiled and went over to her at the sink. "You aren't going to lose me," he said. "I just wish I could give you some comfort."

Her face was pale as she looked at him. "I wish comfort would do some good."

He started to hold her, but her body tensed, and she moved away from him. He thought back to that later, after she had disappeared.

Schafer watched Tom's red shirt move back up through the maze of rocks to the rim. The terrain from that point began its slow rise into the mountain, and now the only obstacles were the small gullies that formed the beginning of the canyon. Schafer followed Tom in the glasses, watching the other man's cursory search. *But he was still looking,* Schafer thought.

Tom walked very slowly, stopping at each boulder and training his binoculars along the hillside. They were fairly close to each other now as the canyon narrowed, and Schafer could see Tom's face through his own glasses. He seemed as hard and as intense as ever, but his movements seemed changed, more deliberate. He took his time now, as though he were tired.

Schafer was disappointed. They had come nearly the whole length of the canyon and now there was no place left to look. The rocks were smaller, not offering either hiding or shade, and it was pointless even to call the boy's name. He moved ahead more rapidly, anxious to meet

Tom and to get the fire started on the mountain. Schafer waited at the head of the canyon.

"What'd you find?" Tom asked when he came up.

"Nothing at all."

"Just as I said from the beginning."

Schafer was sitting down, his pack beside him, looking out at the roseate hills in the distance. Though the ground still radiated warmth, the heat had gone out of the sun, which was far out and flattening against the line of hills to the west. From where he sat, the humpbacked bird looked like two crimson spires, flanked by black robes where the rim of the canyon was buried in shadows. "What about you?" Schafer asked.

"No sign." Tom breathed heavily and took out a hip flask from his pack. "What did you think?"

"I thought you might have found something behind that rock."

"I was taking a crap," Tom said smiling. "I didn't want the boy to see me." He took a shot from the flask and lowered it slowly. "I think the boy's parents were lying."

"What do you mean lying?"

"I don't think there's a soul out here except us. Those people are probably crazier than the boy to begin with. There never was a boy named Joel, much less one that ran away." He stopped suddenly. "Why are you looking at me like that?"

"You found him, didn't you?"

"What?"

"He's dead and you found him," Schafer said.

"If he were found dead," Tom said, "it would have been by the vultures."

Schafer had forgotten the birds. In the open country you knew when something was dead or dying. Tom was right about that. "Why do you think the parents would lie?"

"Maybe they weren't lying," Tom said. He untied the bandana from around his forehead and wiped the dirt from under his eyes. His face seemed darkened after the long day in the sun, and the bandana had made a line across his forehead.

He sat down and let his pack rest against the slope of the hill. "I remember being lost in the hills outside of Sanderson. I was about ten and I was out hunting with my father. He told me to go out and circle around a knoll that he pointed to about a mile away. I thought he was going to watch me, you know, like we were splitting up to chase game to each other. I remember turning back all the time to see whether I could still see him, but even when he had gone I wasn't real scared because I knew he was going to meet me. It wasn't too long until dark, but I figured he knew what he was doing." Tom paused a moment and looked at Schafer. "So I got way the hell over to that knoll, and the whole country was right at my feet, and I'd done what he'd told me. There were a lot of little gullies like the small ones shooting into this canyon right here. But I didn't see my father. I circled around a little, staying around the knoll waiting for him. Then I started getting scared because it was darker then and the snakes would be coming out. So I went back and climbed the knoll and tried to find him. I shouted for him just like you went about shouting for Joel this afternoon. But my father didn't answer either. Finally I got all turned around so that everything looked the same to me, and I panicked and started crying. I wanted him to come and find me, but he didn't. He'd taken off. He must have sent me out there and then just turned around and headed back to the car, because nobody ever saw him again. The sheriff found me the next day, wandering around the tail-end gullies just as I was about to come out onto a dirt road. I knew enough even then to head downhill."

The two men sat a long moment in silence, watching the land change with the ending of the sun. A pair of whitetails made their way over the ridge to their right and picked their way gingerly down the rocky slope toward the river. Tom made no move, and it was Schafer who finally stood up.

He looked back up the barren mountainside where a steep-sloping hill was buttressed by a stand of junipers. "You don't think he would have gone up into the trees?"

"No."

"Well, let's give him a last chance with that fire."

Tom stood up and brushed the dust from his jeans. "We'd better move anyway," he said, taking a last swig from the flask. "The snakes are coming out, and I could use some supper."

The fire swelled against the darkness, and Schafer leaned forward to warm his face. The desert air had cooled rapidly with the darkness and the altitude and the slight breeze that came then off the mountain. Schafer buttoned his jacket all the way up and looked across the fire at Tom, who was finishing the last of his dinner.

Tom's lean features scarcely moved as he ate, and he stared into the fire as though something were sinking in. For a long time he sat without stirring, and then he suddenly shifted.

"What did you hear?" Schafer asked.

Tom's face changed, the veneer giving way to a quick movement of his eyes. He put down his unfinished portion and stood up. "Things are starting to move out there," he said. "The whole land changes."

In the distance a coyote's call went up, an insistent cry that seemed to make Tom wary. It was true, Schafer thought. In the daytime the heat stopped everything, and the animals sought the cool shelter of sand, rock, or yucca. But at night they emerged from that common sleep to prey and be preyed upon, moving through the blackness which protected them.

"Where do you think he is now?" Schafer asked.

Tom pushed back his hat. "He's probably in a nice warm bed."

That thought settled with Schafer. He would have preferred to be in bed himself, and he imagined the boy speaking to his mother from beneath a quilt, just as he remembered that from his own boyhood. In the next room his father was always coughing and spitting and the light that had just been turned off flashed in his eyes. "And keep quiet in there," his father always called out. Schafer had never made any noise.

"Still thinking about Alene?" Tom asked.

"No, I try not to." Schafer looked up, drawn back into the circle of the light with the mention of Alene's name. He kicked a piece of wood in the fire and watched the sparks shoot up in curving patterns into the dark overhead. "I don't know," he said. "I guess I didn't know her well enough."

Tom leaned down and scraped the uneaten food off his plate into the fire. "I didn't think you'd have stayed around so long," Tom said. "I mean, you've been used to moving."

"Leaving gets to be too easy," Schafer answered. "And then, you know, if I left she wouldn't know where to come back."

"What do you mean she left you?" Alene's mother had asked. "Has she been here?"

"I don't think she'd come to us," her father said. "We haven't ever been close."

"Have you been arguing so soon?" her mother put in.

"There was no argument." Schafer had stood on the porch in silence. The west-moving freight was coming in across the curve of the hill, and he watched the white steam rise into the air. Alene would have been able to feel that train, he had thought. The lumbering power of the freight cars seemed to seep through him as it slowed, draining him. The couplings cracked and the high-pitched strain of metal wheels on the track penetrated his brain.

He had stayed up the whole night before, staring at the row of brightly colored dresses that Alene had collected in the closet. He had thought in that first night that she would simply turn around and come back. He would have said nothing against her and asked nothing, because he needed her. But now he could not understand what had happened.

He tried to think of some explanation to give her parents, but nothing came to him. Nothing had gone wrong, and he could think of nothing he had done. All he could think of were good times. He had felt he had finally found his place, and with her he had felt more comfortable than he had ever been in his life.

"Tell us what happened," her mother said.

"I don't know what happened." He had watched the train gathering speed again without stopping, slowing only for the town and then building its momentum on the downhill.

"She's always been like that," her father said. "Always moody and quiet. Ever since junior high school. You could never tell what she was thinking or what she was going to do next."

"The worst of it," Schafer said, "is that I wasn't able to keep her from being what she had always been."

"She isn't coming back," Tom said softly.

"How do you know?"

Schafer looked up at Tom, who had drifted into a serious mood. His eyes were quiet and steady now, as though he had come to some conclusion. "I knew her in Sanderson. Every kid in a small town knows every other kid. She was a real nice girl. You know, quiet."

"I know how she was," Schafer said, feeling the heat rising to his face.

Tom spoke softly. "You just said you didn't know her well enough."

"I don't want to know any more from you."

Schafer started to get up, afraid suddenly of Tom.

"Sit down," Tom said, kneeling himself. He was quiet for a moment, fixing Schafer with a firm look. "Listen to me. Nobody likes what happens in this world. But you can't keep from facing up to things."

"I don't want to face up," Schafer said, his anger starting.

"Neither did I."

Coyotes' calls broke the concentration, and Tom turned in the direction of the sound. "You know what those coyotes are doing?" he asked. "They're ripping up that boy."

"You're lying."

"I wasn't going to tell you," Tom said. "I wasn't going to tell anyone and just let the people suffer. That's what my parents did to me." He let his breath out in a long sigh. "But I can't say he's lost now. He's been found all right, though I didn't want to find him."

"There weren't any vultures," Schafer said.

"Vultures see, they don't smell. I tried to cover the body with rocks in that cave, but the coyotes have found him anyway."

Schafer looked out wildly into the darkness.

"He'd been bitten by rattlers," Tom went on. "Six, seven times in the face. He must have gone into that cave under those big rocks and gone to sleep."

Schafer could hear the yapping and howling, and he stood up and moved a little way from the fire. In the dark he could just make out the spires of the humpbacked bird across the canyon. He had never really cared about the boy, he thought. It was all pretending. Or was it pretending?

He let things settle in his mind. Something had broken loose inside him, the way one of those big rocks washed out of the rim and rolled. "So what is it about Alene?" he asked finally.

Tom spoke in an even, unhurried way, his voice coming from behind Schafer. "When she was fourteen there were a bunch of older boys in Sanderson," he said. "We picked out the shiest, quietest girl we could think of and drove her outside of town into that hill country. I was drawn in with them at first, thinking it was just fun, but when I saw how afraid Alene was, how she didn't even scream when the train came by and the people's faces were pressed against the window." He paused a moment. "I couldn't do it then," he went on. "And I couldn't now."

"Now?"

"At the ranch before she left she came to me," Tom said in a whisper. "Maybe she didn't really want to and something made her. I don't know. She didn't seem to have any purpose. But who knows? Who knows what made that boy run away either."

Shafer half heard. It seemed to him that Tom's voice came from a distance, across some gulf where the voice should not have carried. For Schafer was riding that humpbacked bird, climbing high into the darkness beyond the fire. He stared out a long time, and then he looked back at Tom, who was sitting, bent forward, with his face in his hands.